The Mark

The Mark

JEN NADOL

BLOOMSBURY

NEW YORK BERLIN LONDON

Published by Bloomsbury Books for Young Readers
175 Fifth Avenue, New York, New York 10010

Library of Congress Cataloging-in-Publication Data
Nadol, Jen.
The mark / by Jen Nadol.—1st U.S. ed.
p.   cm.
Summary: While in Kansas living with an aunt she never knew existed and taking a course
in philosophy, sixteen-year-old Cass struggles to learn what, if anything, she should do with
her ability to see people marked to die within a day's time.
ISBN: 978-1-59990-431-3
[1. Psychic ability—Fiction. 2. Death—Fiction. 3. Fate and fatalism—Fiction.
4. Philosophers—Fiction. 5. Orphans—Fiction. 6. Kansas—Fiction.] I. Title.
PZ7.N13353Mar 2010   [Fic]—dc22   2009016974

First U.S. Edition February 2010
Book design by Danielle Delaney
Typeset by Westchester Book Composition
Printed in the U.S.A. by Worldcolor Fairfield, Pennsylvania
2 4 6 8 10 9 7 5 3 1

for my family

The Mark

chapter 1

There is nothing like the gut-hollowing experience of watching someone die, especially when you know it's coming.

I saw the man with the mark at the bus stop on Wilson Boulevard when I crossed Butter Lane on my way to school, the route I took every day. I wanted to look away, pretend he wasn't there, and run for the safety of algebra and honors English, but I didn't. I had promised myself. So I turned right and walked two blocks to the Plexiglas shelter, where we stood silently. It was a misty March day, the chill of winter still in the air. I slid my hand into the outer pocket of my book bag and felt for the change that always jangled around in there. I was counting out eighty-five cents for the ride when he asked, "You know when the B3 comes?"

His skin was smooth and his dark hair threaded with the slightest of gray. He was younger than I'd expected, than I'd have hoped. It limited the possibilities in an unpleasant way. I looked down, trying to ignore the hazy light that surrounded him.

"I think the schedule's on the wall."

"Yeah, I saw it. The bus should have been here five minutes ago." We both turned away, watching the street.

"So you don't know if it's usually late?" he asked without looking back at me.

"No."

He checked his watch, then pulled out a cell phone, exhaled sharply, and put it away. Reception was always lousy here. I pretended to be busy smoothing the folds of my skirt while I watched him from beneath overgrown bangs, glimpses of his ironed trench coat and gleaming shoes filtered as if seen through a bar code. He never glanced my way, but why would he? With my slight frame, I was forever being mistaken as young, but the thrift-store kilt and ponytail I'd worn today probably made me look more like six than sixteen. Hardly worth his notice.

The bus crested the hill finally, *B3 Oak Park* glowing yellow through the light fog. I liked to ride the buses around our little town, just to explore. I walked through neatly groomed neighborhoods or wandered the five square blocks of Ashville center. Some of the shopkeepers knew me: Mr. Williams, the grocer on Spring Street, and Juan at the newsstand. Mostly they ignored me, the way people do who have little interest in anything but getting through the day. But I knew them. I'd watched Mrs. Leshko put out her deli leftovers for the town cats, and Burt Keyes from the convenience store steal extra papers from the Main Street machine.

From my travels, I knew this bus would go through our suburbs into downtown, then to the small communities on the west side. Not that the route mattered. I'd have followed him anywhere.

I sat three rows behind, too nervous to do anything but pick my nails and keep watch. We passed residential streets, under maple trees heavy from the night's rain, adding passengers as we went. When we approached downtown, the man collected his briefcase and umbrella, standing for the Court Street stop. Reluctantly I hefted my bag and followed him off the bus, still nurturing a small hope somewhere that I was wrong.

He walked quickly. I had to trot to keep up, my book bag thumping awkwardly against my back. Without breaking stride he pulled the cell phone from his pocket. I missed his first words in the rush of traffic, but those after were impossible not to hear.

"For crissake, Lorraine! How could the goddamn computer be down?" He paused, stopping short to peer into his briefcase. He'd caught me by surprise and I stopped too, a woman jarring me from behind.

"Sorry," I muttered. She passed, scowling. I shuffled over to the nearest building and leaned against the wall. My backpack, laden with schoolwork I'd slogged through last night for assignments that would now be late, slid to the ground.

"Here it is," he said, yanking a small black book from his bag. He was a rock in the stream of pedestrian traffic, people turning their bodies to slide by with minimum disruption to their morning rush. "Well, that's just great," he said, staring at the opened calendar. "I was due in Judge Shenkman's chambers twenty minutes ago. Why didn't you call . . . Forget it . . ." He tilted his head skyward, searching for rescue from her stupidity. "Just call him now. Explain that my car was broken into. Also, call my wife and remind her to get ahold of the insurance people. And get tech support to fix the damn computer. That's what I pay you for—to manage the details." He snapped the phone shut and thrust it into his pocket.

"Not my fucking day," I heard him mutter as he started walking again.

He had no idea.

At Linden Street, he turned the corner, hurrying toward the rear of the courthouse and the law buildings that surrounded it. I stayed with him, but started to wonder what I'd do when he got to his office or the courthouse. I hadn't really planned this out, but obviously I couldn't follow him in. I'd wait outside, I thought, wishing I had something other than textbooks with me. This could be a long day. I knew I was chicken, but deep down I hoped maybe it would happen inside, somewhere I wasn't allowed.

I needn't have worried. We were at the end of the block, me still trailing a few paces behind. As the man stepped off the curb, I saw the elements coming together—the wet street, his head bent checking the time again, then snapping up at the screech of brakes, a crunch like nothing I've ever heard: of bone and metal and shards of plastic, screams, the people hurrying to work frozen, then running to the street or away from it.

I stood still, book bag at my feet, and forced back dry heaves, thankful I'd skipped breakfast. An ambulance's wail rose over the commotion, the ebb and flow of its siren mournful as it sped the three blocks from Ashville General. EMTs would be on the scene within minutes.

I could have told them not to bother.

chapter 2

I didn't remember getting back on the bus, but rose from my seat by rote as we approached my stop. I stood for a moment, alone in the bus shelter, the rain coming down hard now, and looked at the spot where the man had waited less than an hour ago.

I thought about his people: Lorraine nervously dialing the judge to tell him about her boss's delay, now permanent. His wife, somewhere nearby, maybe on the line with their insurance agent or making coffee or bundling kids off to school, not realizing that all of those things would soon come to a sharp and screeching halt, never to be done with the same emotion again. Then there were his coworkers and the man who sold him coffee or a newspaper or cut his hair—the ripples of his death, any death, stretching on and on.

As I walked home I kept replaying it. Blood and broken glass on the pavement. The wide, unseeing eyes of the man who had hit him and the cell phone spinning brokenly on the shiny asphalt. I didn't know what was worse: what I had seen or what it meant.

Nan was in the living room when I let myself into our apartment. I heard a yoga video and her steady breathing that paused when the door slammed shut behind me.

"Cass, is that you?"

"Yeah." I tossed my bag to the corner near my room, its heavy thud reminding me briefly of school. The thought of going back there after today was both comforting and incomprehensible. The foyer was filled with the sweet, rich smells of cinnamon, allspice, and cloves. Nan was brewing homemade tea—my grandmother, using her own grandmother's Corinthian recipe.

"What are you . . . Oh, sweetie, you're soaked!" I watched Nan's feet as she hurried from the living room across the foyer to where I stood. They were bare, her deep maroon pedicure stark against translucent skin. She cupped my chin and drops of rain—or maybe it was tears—fell onto her wrist.

"What happened?"

I took a breath, cleansing, as her video would say, but my voice still shook. "I saw one today."

She inhaled sharply and seemed almost as afraid to ask as I was to tell; but Nan would never shy away from something that needed doing, no matter how unpleasant. "And?"

I nodded and Nan put her arm around me. "Oh, Cassie. Oh, baby, I'm so sorry." Gently she led me through open French doors into the living room and lowered me to the sofa. The thought crossed my mind that I'd leave a big wet spot on the slipcover, but it didn't bother Nan. She squatted, holding both of my hands in hers, and searched my teary face.

Nan's black eyes were sharp and framed with long lashes, paler now than the charcoal of the faded photo on her dresser. She had once been beautiful—it always surprised me how I could still see it in her face—but it was her spirit, an old friend of hers once told me, more than her exotic Mediterranean looks that had charmed the boys of their childhood neighborhood. Like me, she was short and small-boned but far from frail. There was an unmistakable strength to Nan, both inner and outer. Though her dark hair was now white and her olive skin no longer smooth over prominent cheekbones, Nan was anything but a little old lady.

"Stay here," she said. "I'm going to get you some towels." She crossed the room, deftly turning the TV off and the stereo on, before passing back through the French doors. Mozart played softly. I leaned back, the sofa getting wetter, and let the rising notes from strings, slightly melancholy, wash over me as I tried not to think.

Nan was back a minute later with two fresh Turkish towels, warm from the radiator they'd been draped over, and a change of clothes.

"Here. Dry off; get comfortable while I make you something hot to drink."

Numbly, I stood, undid my ponytail, and dried my straight dark hair, too long and thick for the towel to do more than soak up the heaviest of the rain. I peeled off my dripping clothes, wrapping them in the towel, and slipped on the fleece pants and hoodie Nan had brought, cozy like a hug.

I heard the soft clank of the teapot and mugs, a rush of water, and the closing of cabinet doors in the kitchen. Nan's busyness was soothing, but I knew she was worried. Nan always hummed while she worked, and her silence gave her away.

When she returned a few minutes later, I was tucked into the dry section of the couch. She handed me a steaming mug, keeping one for herself.

"Tea?" I asked.

"With a top hat." All grown-up, she meant. With alcohol. "Sip slowly."

I did. Slowly, but often. She waited until I was halfway through before asking, "Do you want to tell me about it?"

No. But I did anyway. It hurt to talk about it, a clenching in my chest like the heart attack I'd hoped might be the kind of death I'd witness.

Nan and I had known this day was coming, though I think we both wished otherwise. That I'd never see the mark again or it would turn out to be something else—an optical illusion, night blindness, some rare and random problem with my eyes. It had been a presence forever, in my oldest memories, though not many of them. Some years passed when I didn't see it at all. It was only after Nan's last stay in the hospital, more than a year before, that I finally realized what it meant.

As she'd gotten older, Nan's diabetes became less and less manageable at home. We could both handle the drill without panic now: call the ambulance, ride to the hospital, fill out the forms. The nurses knew us and worked quickly to whisk her to the best room available, usually semiprivate. While she was inpatient, I'd take the bus downtown—the B3, as it happens—and walk the few blocks to the hospital.

On the second day of her last lockup, as she called it, I found her reading, lines from her IV draped like ribbons across the bed.

"Hello, sunshine," she whispered. That and the drawn curtain told me Mrs. Gettis in the other bed was sleeping.

"Hello back," I said, pulling over a chair and layering it with pillows to lift me to her level. At five foot one I felt small almost anywhere, but next to the hospital beds on their hydraulic jacks, I could almost inspect the underside of the mattress.

"Are you the princess?" Nan teased, watching me climb onto the stack and sit. "I think housekeeping collected all the peas last night."

"I just don't want you lording over me," I said.

Nan was fine other than feeling like an overloaded pincushion. I told her about my math test—another A—and Spanish paper— only a B. I had almost forgotten about Mrs. Gettis completely until the orderly, Norton, pushed through the door.

"Came to take your roommate for her therapy," he said, nodding at Nan with a smile.

He disappeared behind the curtain and Nan and I paused, knowing it was rude to eavesdrop, but suddenly reminded that we weren't at home. Mrs. Gettis snorted awake, groaning at Norton's urging to get up, help him move her to the wheelchair. Mrs. G. also had a chronic condition—bronchitis or asthma, something like that. Not serious, just a nuisance like Nan's diabetes. But when Norton wheeled her out, both of them waving briefly as they passed, I saw it. The mark.

It's like the haze at the edge of a flame or the glow of a lightbulb through fog. Constant and surrounding, but not obscuring. I could see Mrs. Gettis perfectly. She wasn't blurry or misty, but she was outlined with a soft luminance.

"What is it?" Nan asked. I'd been staring after them.

I shook my head, smiled, and turned back to her. "Nothing."

When I walked into Nan's room the next day, the curtain was pushed back, sunlight spilling through the plate glass window and across the neatly made second bed. I think it started to connect then because I felt a heaviness in my gut that shouldn't have been. It was a perfect day. I'd aced my history test and even found an extra five in my backpack on the way to the hospital.

"Mrs. Gettis check out?" I tried to keep the quaver from my voice because even as I asked it, I could read the answer on Nan's face.

"No, Cassie. She had a heart attack yesterday."

"Oh no."

Nan nodded. "She didn't make it." I could feel her watching me, but couldn't meet her eyes, could barely keep myself upright. "Cassie? Cass?" I nodded, trying to get it together. "Are you okay?" I nodded again, but it was unconvincing. "Should I call a nurse, sweetheart?"

"No."

"Honey, you're completely pale. Sit down." It was a good idea, and I sank into the chair I'd piled pillows on just the day before, gripping its wood armrests tightly. Nan was still watching me, her eyes intense, probing. Her brow was furrowed above that strong, patrician nose, undeniably Greek like my own. I could sense her trying to figure out how to help with her stuck in the bed and me in the chair.

"I'm sorry, Cassie. I didn't know you'd be so upset or I'd have called you before . . ."

"No, it's okay."

"Death is always hard."

Well, she was right about that.

Mrs. Gettis had been the first clue, eventually leading me to today. The man I'd followed, the nail in the coffin, so to speak.

"So, now you know," Nan said as we sat snuggled on the sofa, cupping our mugs, both of us calmer than we should be. Maybe it was shock. Outside, rain pelted the roof and window, adding percussion to our Mozart.

Then Nan asked the question I knew was coming, the one I'd been asking myself since the squeal of tires burned themselves into my brain. "What now?"

I wasn't in a good mood, but I couldn't help a small smile. It was her trademark question. Even if Nan had ideas—and she always did—she made me figure things out myself first. She was big into personal accountability. No lesson like one learned the hard way, she often told me.

I didn't answer. I don't think she really expected me to.

Through the rest of the day, Nan tried to keep my mind off it—we played Yahtzee and Scrabble, watched *Annie Hall*, and skipped the news. But in the down moments, and especially when I finally climbed into bed after eleven, my body too worn out to keep up with my feverish brain, I couldn't stop replaying the scene. Watching him climb off the bus, dial the cell phone, look at his watch, step off that curb, over and over. The visions swirled in sequence, then out, linked by a final haunting question. Could I have prevented it?

chapter 3

"Who was the first woman appointed to the Supreme Court?" Mr. Dempsey ignored my raised hand, scanning the room. When no one else volunteered, he pointed to me. "Yes, Cassie?"

"Sandra Day O'Connor."

Mr. Dempsey nodded and Ally Drewnate marked another chalk stroke for our team.

"What was the Zapruder film?"

No hands went up. Hadn't anyone seen *JFK*? Nan loved a good conspiracy theory.

"No one?" Mr. Dempsey looked at me. A couple people on my team did too. I shrugged and shook my head. No point in being a show-off.

This was my favorite kind of history class, when Mr. Dempsey ditched the textbook, the *Dictionary of Cultural Literacy* propped open on his desk instead.

Across the room, Val Wertz eyed the clock. There was a pep rally instead of fifth period today, and she and the other cheerleaders probably couldn't wait. I was looking forward to it myself; I had *The Stand* in my backpack. My third time reading it, but Stephen King never gets old.

The bell interrupted Mr. Dempsey's explanation of the assassination caught on tape.

"Team A wins," he called while the class filed toward the door. "Thirty-two to seventeen."

"Cassie does it again," Jack Petroski said, looking over his shoulder to smile at me as he steered Val through the door.

"Nice going, Cass," Val agreed. Jack had his arm around her.

I shrugged, trying to ignore the twinge I felt watching them. Watching him. "A team effort."

Jack snickered.

"Good luck, Val," I said gamely, waving as I turned down the hallway toward my locker. Val and I weren't buddies, but there were few people in our class of forty-six who weren't friendly with each other. Ashville High was too small for battle lines between cheerleaders and nerds, preps and emos. We barely had enough kids to fill the categories.

As I twirled the combination of my lock, Tasha Lusetovich sauntered down the hall, her dark glossy hair pulled away from her face by a blue bandanna. On anyone else, it would have looked like they'd just finished at their uncle's farm, but on Tasha it was somehow elegant. Like everything she wore. Tasha and I had been fast friends when she'd moved to our small Pennsylvania town from New York two years before. I'd known as soon as I saw her sitting alone on the steps, waiting for the doors of her new school to open, that she'd be interesting. She had ignored all the chattering around her, her nose buried in a thick paperback that turned out to be John Irving. My kind of chick. But Tasha and I weren't close enough that I'd told her about Robert McKenzie. Only Nan was close enough for that.

Of course I'd looked him up. The dead man. I followed every newspaper article for the week after, until his name, his photos, his life faded from the daily events. Nan neither encouraged nor discouraged me, picking up papers from the supermarket upon request. We didn't talk about it, but I saw her reading them late at night, her soft white hair fuzzy around the hand that propped her cheek.

He was forty-one years old. One child: a daughter. That part hurt. God knows I knew what she was going through, my own parents killed in a car accident when I was two.

The McKenzies lived in a brick house, ostentatious with white columns and clipped hedges. It was on our side of town, but too far from the apartment to walk. I rode my bike instead, leaning it against a No Parking sign while I pretended to tie my shoe across the street. The curtains were drawn and there was a museum-like quality to the house. Silent. Frozen in time.

I thought about him a lot: about where his life might have gone, where his daughter's, his wife's would go now. It was tough to get that day out of my head, even standing in the shiny school hallway two months later.

"Earth to Renfield," Tasha said, poking my shoulder.

"Hey." I tossed my history book into the locker. "What's up?"

She shrugged. "*Nada mucho.* You coming over today?"

"Yeah." I shut the locker and we started down the hall toward the auditorium. "I'll definitely need to wear the guard, though." I held out my arm and pushed back the sleeve. "The inside of my elbow is raw."

"Wimp."

We had found Tasha's dad's bow and arrows a couple weeks ago, poking around her attic one afternoon. Instead of telling us to stay out of his stuff, her dad had bought a target and some bales of hay and set up a practice range for us in their garage. I liked the feel of the bow in my arms, curving protectively above and below me, like a shield. I was getting pretty good, even better than Tasha, who I was pretty sure was practicing on the sly.

We had almost reached the double steel doors to the auditorium when the PA crackled my name: "Cassandra Renfield to the main office, please."

Tasha and I exchanged a look. "Want me to come?" she asked.

"Nah. Go on in. Save me a seat." I kept my voice light, though I doubted I'd make it to the assembly.

I was right. The cement of the school steps was warm on my legs as I sat in the bright sun. Nan was in the hospital again, Principal McCarthy's assistant had told me. I'd suspected as much.

I could hear the *boom-boom-boom* of the bass drum and crash of cymbals from the auditorium while I waited for my cab. "I already called," the assistant had said when I asked about getting one. "It should be here any minute." Which would be accurate if she really meant any minute twenty minutes from now. Taxis in Ashville were notoriously slow. Nan would be in her room by the time I got there, hooked up to the IVs and drips that stabilized her blood sugar, bringing her back to herself.

A school bus turned the corner I'd been watching for my cab, slowly cruising toward me. I looked away. I hadn't ridden one in years and wouldn't mind if I never did again. They'd never bothered me before Mrs. Gettis, but now they reminded me of the West

Lakes kids, the link between her and Mr. McKenzie that made me nearly certain what I'd see when I followed him two months ago.

When Nan told me about Mrs. Gettis that day at the hospital, I knew almost immediately where I needed to go. She'd wanted me to stay. Rest. Of course, the only other bed was Mrs. G.'s, which wasn't going to fly.

It was a quick walk to the main branch of the Ashville Library, one I barely remembered, my mind utterly consumed with Mrs. Gettis and a much older memory.

"I'd like to see papers from a while back," I told the librarian. "Around ten or eleven years ago, I think."

"Those would still be on microfilm," the librarian answered. "We're scanning everything into computers, but it's going very slowly. All the film is in the basement."

It took me nearly two hours to find what I was looking for. I knew it was spring or fall, warm outside, but that still left a lot of days. When the front page flashed on the backlit screen, I knew right away that I'd found it. The school looked exactly as I'd remembered. Staring at the headline, I realized that I could have asked the librarian when it had happened. She'd have known in an instant, but I was glad I hadn't. I didn't want to hear her memories. I wanted to focus on my own.

SCHOOL BUS CRASH KILLS TWELVE

A school bus carrying 26 West Lakes Elementary School students plunged 40 feet off the side of a highway overpass Monday in Gideon, killing at least 12 children, according to school, police and fire officials.

A witness told police it appeared that a small car struck the bus, which then went over the guardrail of Interstate 565, crashing onto Church Street.

Police are attempting to find the driver of the car. It took authorities about an hour to transport the 26 students and the bus driver to Gideon Hospital, police officer Richard Johnson said.

The emergency room was overwhelmed. "It was a very chaotic scene and parents were just frantic," Johnson said. "Gideon has never seen an accident like this involving students."

He noted that the bus—like nearly all school buses—was not equipped with adequate seat belts or air bags.

Nan and I had "gone visiting" that day, eleven years before, bringing food to a housebound woman who lived outside town. I'd tried to keep up with Nan over block after block, hot in my wool coat. It was too tight, pinning my arms when I tried to swing them all the way front.

"Come on, Cassie." Nan turned and waited for me to catch up. I could hear the shouts of children ahead. Inside the chain-link fence surrounding the school yard, sun glinted off the slide and swing chains rattled. I was about to ask Nan if we could stop there after visiting the lady's house, when I saw them: the glowing kids. There was a whole group together, bouncing a red rubber ball. Kids not so much bigger than me. My eyes swept the playground, seeing a few more: one on the swings. One running and laughing. One sitting alone, back against the school wall. I stared, not realizing I'd stopped until Nan called from the end of the block.

"Cassie! Come *on*." I ran to her, my shoes slap-slapping on the sidewalk. "Let's deliver this food, hon, before it starts to go bad."

Nan grasped my hand, her fingers firm around my wrist, and started to walk.

"Why are those kids lit up?"

She hesitated, frowning and looking down at me. "What kids?"

"Back there." I pointed to the playground.

Nan turned, dropping my hand to shade her eyes. "What do you mean 'lit up'?" She searched the playground slowly before turning back to me. "You mean by the sun?"

I shrugged. It wasn't the sun. Some were in the shadow of the school building and some weren't, but they all looked the same. Even from far away I could see the light around them, like a candle with something hiding just the flame.

Nan glanced at the school again, her eyes narrowed, searching. "I don't see anything, Cass. How are they 'lit up'?"

But I didn't have the words, and anyway, I think I knew she didn't see it. "Can we go to that playground after?" I asked instead.

Nan reached for my hand again and we crossed the street. "I don't think so, sweetie. It's for the school. Maybe we can find another one."

I don't remember if we went to a playground later or not, but I remember those kids. It was the kind of thing that sticks with you, maybe my earliest memory. I was four.

I'd left the library in a daze, trying hard not to think about the mark, forcing away the terrible suspicion of what it was. I'd waited until Nan was discharged from the hospital to tell her. It would be easier in the security of our home, I'd thought. Plus, I needed a few days to sort it out, make sure I wasn't crazy or delusional, though I couldn't really think of a way to explain it without sounding like one or both. I was going to let Nan settle in, unpack, have some tea or whatever, but as soon as the apartment door closed behind us, she said, "So, are you going to tell me what's up?"

"What do you mean?" I looked down, shuffling the mail that I'd organized the day before.

"You've been distracted for days, Cassie. Is something wrong at school?"

"No."

"Then what?" She stood, arms akimbo, more like a drill sergeant than a convalescent.

I nodded, at a total loss for how to start. "Do you remember the bus accident that happened in Gideon a while back?" I finally asked. "The one with a bunch of West Lakes Elementary School kids?"

Nan nodded. "I do. It was about eight or nine years ago."

"Eleven," I corrected.

"Could be," she agreed slowly, her eyes faraway.

"We passed that school the day it happened."

"I remember," she said. "We were going to Miss Loretta's house. Do you remember her?"

"Not really."

"We were there three or four times to bring her food or groceries, sometimes just to visit. You loved the figurines she kept by the window." Images of delicate, lacy castles and cats ran through my mind as Nan looked back at me. "What about the accident?"

"There were children playing outside when we passed the school," I reminded her. "I saw something." I stopped, trying to find the right words. "A light, kind of a glow, around them. Not all of them, but a bunch. About twelve."

Though her expression didn't change, there was a sharpening in her dark eyes. Recognition.

"I saw the same thing this week at the hospital. On Mrs. Gettis when Norton wheeled her out of the room." I paused and, just to be clear, added, "The day she died."

Nan bit her lip and I heard her sharp intake of breath, breaking the silence in the apartment. Her hands had fallen to the side, no longer on her hips, but dangling impotently. We were still in the foyer and I wished we'd made it to the living room, because Nan looked drained, as if her body might sink to the floor. When she spoke, though, her voice was calm. Quiet, but strong. "What are you saying, Cassie?"

I shrugged, though there wasn't much uncertainty about it. "I'm saying . . . that I think I see something—this mark—when someone is about to die."

She nodded slowly as if this crazy, awful thing I'd told her was perfectly normal. Then Nan crossed the foyer in two sure steps and gave me a hug. "Come," she said, typically Nan. "Help me make some tea."

It was a huge relief to have said it, my body feeling physically weakened. I'd known Nan would listen, she always did, but still I'd been afraid. This was much different from telling her I'd failed a test or thought the kids' charity she'd donated to was a fraud. Those things might upset her, but at least they were believable.

We purposely talked of the everyday while we worked; Nan asked about the neighbors, the mail, my tests and papers. It wasn't until we were in our usual spots on the sofa that we went back to it. Nan's legs were curled close to her body. She always sat that way, snuggled up against herself, her body leaving a permanent imprint on the cushion.

"I remember that day," she said, cupping her mug. "We got lost. That's why we passed West Lakes. You asked me something about the kids, something odd."

I nodded, sipping my tea for distraction.

"Tell me about it, Cassie." She waited without the slightest hint of anxiety or eagerness or fear. She was like this in everything. And only because of that could I share the implausible, the impossible.

"There's not much to tell, not much more than I've already said." I took a deep breath, trying again to find the right words. "It's a light, a glow. Like an outline around the person."

"Bright?"

I pictured Mrs. Gettis rolling past us in her wheelchair, before shaking my head. "Not so that it's hard to look at. More . . . constant, I guess. Not a glare."

"Not a reflection? Like the sun off metal?"

"No. But it also doesn't come from within the person. It's not like they're glowing, exactly . . ." It sounded ridiculous. "More like they're standing in front of something lit and I can see its glow around them. But when they move, the light always stays behind them." I shook my head and said what I knew Nan was thinking: "It sounds crazy."

"It does," she agreed, "but you're not the crazy type, Cass. There have been others? Besides Mrs. G. and the kids?"

I nodded.

"A lot?"

"Not a lot. But enough." More than enough, now that I knew what it meant. Nan waited, sipping her tea, her eyes never leaving mine. "The last one before Mrs. Gettis was a year or two ago. We were driving through town, going to the mall, I think. She was old, sitting on a bench. It was quick, I barely saw her."

"And before that?"

"I don't know. It seems like there's always such a long stretch between. I haven't paid that much attention." Even as I said it, though, I could see them flashing before me: a young mother pushing a stroller, a man in a wheelchair, a couple kissing before they got in their car. Years of them imprinted on my brain.

"You're sure that's what it means?" she asked.

"No." How could anyone be sure of something so outlandish? "But I think it's a possibility. A very real one. What else could it be?"

We finished our tea, neither of us answering my question with the obvious response that it could be anything. Anything would be more likely than what I'd told her. It wasn't until we put our mugs down that Nan broke the silence.

"So, what now?"

"I don't know," I had answered. "I need to think about it." But the idea had already formed. I knew what I needed to do and the next day, I told Nan my plan. The one that had led me to Mr. McKenzie.

Looking back, it seems weird that I didn't question more—before Mrs. Gettis and Mr. McKenzie—what the mark meant or why I saw it. I guess it's like hearing a strange noise or seeing a flash of lightning. You hold your breath until it happens again. And again. Each time you get closer to pinpointing its origin. I had seen the mark a handful of times in my life. Sometimes no more than a passing glimpse, like the old woman on the bench. The sightings were never close enough to link one to the next or discern a pattern. It itched at me a little more every time, but that nagging feeling always dissipated as days passed. It was a small idiosyncrasy in my life back then. Maybe there was a why and maybe not. It didn't really matter.

A car turned onto my street, following the path the school bus had taken fifteen minutes before. I squinted, just able to make out writing on the side. Had to be my cab. Finally.

"Ashville General, please," I told the driver as I climbed in, headed back to the hospital where I'd finally put it all together— what the mark meant.

He nodded. "The lady told me when she called. Your grand-mother's sick, huh?"

I should have been annoyed, but I knew the principal's assis-tant only meant well. I could almost hear the conversation: poor dear, no other family, such a burden, don't let her brood.

"Yeah, diabetes. No big deal, just a hassle to keep up with sometimes."

"My brother-in-law's uncle had it. Always shootin' up with the needles."

He had the accent of somewhere else, but I didn't feel like ask-ing about it. Or talking about the uncle. "Uh-huh."

Ashville slid past us, a blur of new leaves, bright sky, and solid family homes. We were at the hospital within fifteen minutes.

Nan was sleeping when I entered the room. She was propped against a pile of pillows and I could hear the faintest of snores. There were three IVs by her side, their needles jabbed into her bony arm. She looked gray, as she often did when these episodes started. And she looked old, partly because we were in a hospital, but mostly just because she was.

"I'm here, Nan," I whispered, placing my hand gently on her free arm. "I'm going to the nurses' station for a few minutes, but I'll be right back."

Tina was on, as I hoped she'd be.

"Sucks to see you," I greeted her.

"Same." She smiled gently, her dusky skin radiant, even under the hospital's fluorescent lights. "How are you, Cass?"

"Fine. How's Nan?"

"Pretty much the usual. We've run her sugars, given her insulin. We should have the labs back in"—she checked the wall clock—"another twenty minutes or so."

I nodded. "I didn't see another bed in there. She have her own room this time?"

"Yeah. She called after last time and arranged for a private room, space permitting."

I thought about that for a minute and knew Nan had done it for me. Not wanting me to see another Mrs. Gettis here. She hadn't mentioned anything.

"Okay, well, I'll be in with her. She's sleeping now, but I want to be there when she wakes up."

"It might be a little while, we gave her a sedative. She needed some rest."

"I've got a book."

I settled into the tan chair near the window in her room, shifting my weight carefully so the plastic wouldn't make those squeaky noises that sound like farts. Nan stirred and muttered something, but it was nearly an hour later when she finally woke.

"Fancy meeting you here," she said, her voice cracking. She reached for the water by her bedside, but the IV lines held her back.

I got up and handed her the glass. "What's a nice gal like you doing in a place like this?"

She drank deeply. "I could ask you the same thing."

"How're you feeling, Nan?"

"Fabulous."

"Tina stopped in, said the labs look good."

"How long have you been here?"

"An hour or so. You weren't out that long."

"I feel like I still am. They must have given me a horse tranquilizer."

I nodded. "She didn't say what it was."

Nan sighed. "So what did I pull you away from at school?"

"Nothing. Literally. I was on my way to a pep rally to read a little Stephen King. It was much quieter here."

Nan nodded and glanced out the window, her face already more vivid. It seemed like she might climb out of bed and start her yoga as she did every morning. As she probably had this morning before whatever happened, happened.

"Did you use the call button?"

She shook her head. "No. I was with Agnes. Meals-on-Wheels day. We were waiting for her nephew John to take us to the Volunteer Center, but I must have passed out first. I just remember seeing those angels she has painted on her ceiling, then I was being lifted out of there, into the ambulance. Nan-on-Wheels."

"So Agnes called school?"

"I guess. She's almost part of the routine now, huh?" This was the third time Agnes had been there for an episode. No surprise. She lived across the street, and she and Nan were wearing a path in the blacktop from their trips back and forth.

I stayed with Nan through dinner. Her doctor did more blood work—her sugars were stabilizing slower than normal and he wanted to be sure she was A-okay before leaving. Finally, around nine she sent me packing.

"You've got school tomorrow, Cass. I don't want you missing another day."

I nodded. "I'll come by after classes. Tell them I'll have the filet for dinner."

"I'm sure they'll bring it with my Chianti. Scoot."

I fell asleep in the cab ride home, dreaming of Agnes's frescoed angels drinking wine.

chapter 4

"Was it Nan?" Tasha was waiting at my locker when I jogged in just before the first bell. There had been two messages on the machine when I got back to the apartment and three on my cell, but I was too beat to call her back.

"Yeah. She's fine." We were hustling to algebra for a test I hadn't spent nearly enough time studying for. I'd squeezed in about thirty minutes at the hospital and probably another ten at home before I fell asleep. The sharp corner of the book was jabbing my leg when I woke up.

"She getting out today?"

I shook my head. "Tomorrow."

"Want me to come to the hospital with you?"

"Nah, it's horribly boring." Tasha nodded. She had gone with me before. "But thanks for offering. What'd I miss at assembly yesterday?"

"What do you think you missed?"

"Nothing?"

"Bingo," she whispered as we slid into our seats.

I bombed the exam. Algebraic formulas kept slipping from my mind like buttery noodles. I knew Mr. Manus would give me a break if I told him about Nan, but I hoped I had done well enough to at least pass. My average was high enough to take a hit or two.

I took the bus downtown after school. Tina and I had talked at lunch. She'd said everything looked good for Nan's release the next day. I would take the morning off from school to go with Agnes and John for the discharge. What a party. We called John a lot after Nan had donated her car to Heritage for the Blind when the doctor said she couldn't drive anymore. She'd regretted it almost immediately, thinking she should have saved it for me.

"I don't need a car," I'd told her. "I like the bus. You see more." Of course, that was before I understood some of what I was seeing. I'd noticed that lately I'd been more inclined to read or pick my fingernails or study the floor as I rode. Just in case.

I got off the B3 before Court Street, avoiding Robert McKenzie's corner. It was three short blocks to the hospital if I cut across the main square, one of my favorite places to hang out in town: great people-watching, brick sidewalks, cool shops. It'd be corny to say I could hear birds in the air and smell spring as I crossed through, but I did. That's what I loved about the smallness of Ashville, even the most down parts of downtown were clean and friendly, safe for me to wander on my own, day or night.

A block off the square, I passed through the doors of Ashville General, trading the smells of outside for antiseptic and air-conditioning. Tina wasn't at the nurses' station on Nan's floor, though I knew she was still on. I headed for room 316, the last on the right with a nice view of downtown through the window.

I walked into Nan's room, ready to tell her about the beautiful day and my lousy math test, but all of this—everything— evaporated into empty nothingness when I looked at her.

"Hi Cassie," Nan said, the words fading when she saw my face. If she could, she'd have rushed to my side, given me a hug, and held me up as she had the day I came home dripping wet after watching Robert McKenzie get run over. But she couldn't because she was attached to cords and wires and tubes that I suddenly knew were useless. "Cassie, what's wrong?"

I couldn't answer. There was no voice, no words to tell her.

"Cassie?" There was a change, the start of understanding. "Are you okay?"

I nodded and closed my eyes, rubbing them with my forefinger and thumb, not surprised to find them come away covered with tears.

"You see it, don't you?" It was barely a question.

I wanted to go to her, but I was afraid to get closer, to touch the luminous haze. I stared at my hands gripping each other tightly, but I couldn't feel the pressure that caused blood to pool at each fingertip.

Then she spoke, her voice steady and comforting. Soft. That made it worse, the knowledge that even now Nan was my rock and that tomorrow, I'd be all alone. "It's okay, Cassie. It was only a matter of time, sweetheart."

I nodded, still unable to look at her. It wasn't okay. Not even a little bit. "I should go . . . find Tina . . . or the doctor. Tell them . . ." My brain struggled for the right action. "Tell them something's wrong."

In the two months since Robert McKenzie's accident, I'd been able to grasp the reality of that day, but not tackle the question that had begun to form as I watched him step off the curb. There would never be a better chance than now. We were in a hospital, for God's sake. And there was no one more important to me than Nan. I said it again, more decisively: "I'm going to get help."

"Do you think there's anything they can do?" Nan was so matter-of-fact. As if we were talking about something as trivial as improving my archery shot or making tea.

"I don't know," I answered honestly, but it was the small glimpse of hope that kept me sane. "Maybe."

"Go see them, then. But, Cassie," she cautioned, "think about what you want to say."

I left the room, more determined with each step. There might not be much time. I had to find someone fast. Thankfully, I saw Tina leaving a patient's room. I ran to her.

"Tina, I'm worried about Nan," I blurted, grabbing her arm to pull her back toward Nan's room.

She sped up. I could feel her muscles tense. "What happened?"

"I don't know. I just . . ." I remembered Nan's warning, but I had to make Tina understand. "I have a really bad feeling. Something's going to happen." She slowed, just a fraction of a step, but hesitation, any hesitation, could be devastating. I stopped and grabbed her arms above the elbows, firmly enough that she winced. "Tina, trust me. You know I'm not the hysterical type." My voice was steady and deadly serious. "I sometimes have a sixth sense about this kind of thing. Something isn't right. I don't know what, but can we please check Nan, go over her charts, get Dr. Wentworth. Something bad is going to happen." I couldn't stop my voice from breaking on the last sentence, and I think Tina, who had never seen me cry, was scared enough that even if she didn't believe me, believed it was worth humoring me.

"Okay, Cassie," she said, gently shaking free of my grip. "Let's go see her."

"Thank you," I whispered.

Nan was unchanged when we got to her room. Still propped in bed, staring out the window. Quiet. Still glowing.

"Miss Nan? How are you feeling? Cassie said something's wrong."

Nan looked at me before answering. "I feel fine, really. Not much different than yesterday."

"I told Tina that I had a bad feeling and that I sometimes have a sense about these things," I added quickly.

"That she does," Nan agreed.

Tina looked at the two of us, trying to reconcile it all: my panic, Nan's calm, the apparent lack of a problem. "Well," she said slowly, "we could rerun your blood work, just to see if anything looks amiss. But I'll have to get Dr. Wentworth's approval, and your insurance might not cover it."

"Fine," I said. "Let's do it. How long will it take?"

"I'll try to get him on the phone now." Tina glanced at the clock on her way out. "He's probably still in the hospital."

Alone, Nan and I stared out the window. I felt better for doing *something*, but then I looked at her, saw the hazy glow, and tensed up all over again.

"How do you feel, Nan? Really?"

She shrugged. "Not like I'm at death's door."

"But something doesn't feel right, does it?"

She shrugged again.

"Nan." I tried to get through to her. "You have to tell me. You have to tell the doctor. You know what it means, what I'm seeing. How can you hold back?"

"There's not much to tell, Cassie. I've got a little indigestion. Otherwise I feel perfectly fine. I'm in the hospital, they've run a thousand and one tests on me, they're about to run even more. If they can't find anything, what can we do?"

I was getting angry. And starting to wonder if Nan really believed me. "How can you be so nonchalant?"

"Maybe because I believe if it's my time, it's my time."

Tina came back then. "Dr. Wentworth is in the middle of a case, but he gave me the go-ahead to run some tests." Silently she drew the blood, five or six vials from Nan's already depleted right arm. "He'll be up when we get the results." She turned at the door, adding, "I'll be at the station. Call me if you need anything."

The waiting had begun. I didn't know what to do with myself and walked to the window, my stomach sour and nerves hair-trigger tense. Outside, the sky was still blue, I'm sure birds were still singing and the air still smelled warm and fertile. I didn't give a damn about any of it. It looked surreal, like a painting or a stage set.

"Cassie, come. Sit with me." Nan's voice, still soft, still calm, brought me back to the room. Mechanically I obeyed, pulling a chair to her side, piling it with pillows as I did every time we sat together like this in the hospital. Me by her bedside. "You know what I was remembering this morning?"

"What?"

"The day your mother first brought you to meet me." Nan shook her head, smiling. "They drove all day for two days, her and your father, sixteen hours from Bering, Kansas, in his new Chrysler." Nan added softly, "God, he loved that car."

I couldn't believe Nan wanted to talk about this right now. I bit my tongue and nodded.

"It was a day very much like today. Sunny, mid-spring, just starting to warm. It is warm out today, right?"

"Yes." It was strange to think that to Nan, it could be twenty or eighty degrees outside and the sky and clouds would look the same. She hadn't been out today, hadn't felt the breeze, smelled the dirt. Maybe never would again. It made me want to run from the room and find a wheelchair or, the hell with it, push her out there, bed and all. But we couldn't leave. Not until we saw the doctor and the results.

"In fact, it may well have been today," Nan was saying. "It would have been about this time of year. You had just turned five months old."

"That's the first time you met me?"

"I know. It seems odd, doesn't it? But your father, Daniel, was tied up with his job at the university, couldn't take enough leave to come. And Georgia didn't want to make such a long trip alone. Looking back, it seems remiss of me not to have visited them to see my first, my only grandchild. Of course, in retrospect, I wished I'd gone out more not just to see you, but to see her."

Clumsily Nan reached for the water on her nightstand. I started to help her, but she waved me away, carefully clutching the glass in her veined hand.

"You were such a beautiful family, standing at my doorstep. Georgia's hair was just like yours, nearly black, almost blue in the sunlight. You were so little, Cass. It was silly, and I never said it to Georgia, but I felt like I could see myself in you. Even that early on."

Another time, I'd have been fascinated by this conversation. I knew so little about my parents, their faces only photographs, their voices, their touch imagined. Nan rarely talked about them— I could tell it was hard for her—but I didn't really want to hear about them now. My insides were churning and I was as jittery as if I'd been mainlining coffee.

"You only stayed the weekend," Nan went on. "Four days of driving for just two days of visit. My fault again, I'm sure. Back at work on Monday, wouldn't dream of taking time off. Not even for my daughter." She shook her head and, for me too, it was hard to believe. So unlike the Nan I knew.

"And the next time I saw you," she said, "was in Kansas. You were two, no longer a baby. I was there to bury your . . . parents. And to bring you home."

"That must have been terrible, Nan."

She nodded. "It was. It was so unreal, a jumble from the minute I got the call about the crash. Some of it I barely remember and some is . . . unforgettable."

"And then, after that, we came back here. You and me?"

"As quickly as we could. Once I'd made up my mind to take you in, I wanted it done. Wanted away from that town. There was some talk of Daniel's parents raising you out there, but Paula— Daniel's mom—knew she couldn't take you in right then as sick as her husband was. They must have hated seeing you leave with a virtual stranger. We'd talked about my bringing you back after her husband passed. She knew it was coming. But I don't think she knew what a toll it would take on her. She was gone by the year's end."

"So you were stuck with me then."

She smiled. "I was. And by that point, there wasn't a chance in hell I'd have given you up."

Nan and I were startled by the soft whisper of the door opening. Tina stuck her head in. "Dr. Wentworth's on his way with the labs."

My stomach rolled. I hadn't forgotten what we were waiting for or what the soft glow around Nan meant, but listening to her had taken my mind off it for at least those few minutes. In my lap, my hands were clasped, as if by holding firmly to each other they could keep today, tomorrow, all my days from unraveling as I was sure they soon would.

Nan kept right on talking as if Tina had just popped in to say lunch was coming. "I was a different person before you came to me," Nan said, her voice still calm and assured, but sad too. "Maybe not a very likable one. So much changed after the accident. After Georgia died. Every day I wish I could have her back, but then I get to thinking what I was like before and wonder if it would have mattered anyway. Would I ever have gotten around to visiting more? Telling her how much I loved her? If she had lived, I'm sure you and I never would have been as close as we are, Cassie. Not that I am ever, for a minute, glad that Georgia is gone, but having you has been the best part of my life. Has, I believe, made all the difference in these last fourteen years being happy ones or not."

She stopped and, though it was my turn to speak, I was without words. Nan didn't seem to mind. She looked away, clearly still thinking about her daughter. My mother.

"The thing is, Cass . . . and you know this about me . . . I believe things take their own course, happen for a reason. I wasn't always that way. Used to think I could control everything. I'm much happier for having stopped trying."

I knew what Nan was doing. I thought about calling her on it, but she was good, distracting me with talk of my mother, inevitables. Still, I knew she had started to say her good-byes.

Dr. Wentworth came in then, his head bent, showing us only the thick gray hair that always stayed rigidly in place. He held a clipboard and his gaze was fixed on it rather than meeting our eyes.

"We've rerun all of your core tests, Ms. Dinakis. And, aside from a slightly elevated blood pressure, they're fine."

"That can't be," I said. "You've missed something."

He looked up at me, his steely eyes emotionless, used to handling the irrational. "Why do you say that?"

"Something's wrong. I know it is. What about her blood pressure?"

Dr. Wentworth glanced at his papers again and shrugged. "It's elevated, but not enough for concern. It's not unusual after an episode like your grandmother had."

I shook my head. "Then it must be something else. What other tests are there?"

Dr. Wentworth turned to Nan. "Is there something you're not telling me?"

Nan shrugged and before she could answer, I butted in. "Listen, I . . . I don't know how to explain it, but I have a sense about this kind of stuff sometimes. About bad things . . ." I could hear desperation, a whiny, pleading thread in my voice. How could I tell him? If I explained, he'd never believe me. If I didn't, he'd think just what I could see written all over his face: that I was a hysterical girl, maybe a touch crazy.

Nan said Dr. Wentworth was a good doctor, so I'd ignored the way he talked to me like I was a five-year-old and never looked me in the eye. But obviously he wasn't a good *enough* doctor, because he didn't know something was wrong and I did. Except I couldn't tell him how. I felt like screaming, I was so frustrated, and I had to grit my teeth as I watched him suppress a grin.

"You mean like a sixth sense?"

I stared right back at him. "Something like that."

He stole a quick look at Nan, then Tina. Seeing no humor in either of their faces, he composed himself. "I know how upsetting it is to have someone you love in the hospital like this. It's natural to be worried, even think that the worst is just around the corner, but your grandmother is fine. Really."

I was waiting for him to come put his arm around me, but to his credit, he stood his ground. At least he could read me that well. There wasn't a chance I was letting him off with a bunch of platitudes, though. "Here's the thing . . . ," I said, trying to figure out a way to frame it.

"Cassie," Nan interrupted. "Leave it." She turned to Dr. Wentworth and Tina. "May we have a few minutes alone?"

"Of course," Dr. Wentworth said. He patted my shoulder, his big hand heavy on the tender spot where my backpack always rested. "It's going to be okay."

"Don't leave," I said, my voice low so Nan couldn't hear, but urgent. "Please. I still need to talk to you."

He patted my shoulder again without answering.

When the door hissed softly closed, Nan asked, "How were you going to explain it, Cassie?"

"I don't know. I'd figure something out. It's better than just letting him go like that." I waved toward the door. "He could be leaving the hospital now. And we need him." I was ready to run after him and actually took a step in that direction, but Nan kept pressing.

"For what?"

"To figure out what's wrong. What's going to happen."

"Why?"

"Why?" How could she ask that? "Because I know and you know, if you believe me, that something's going to happen to you. Something bad that will . . . that . . ."

She nodded. "That could be the end."

"Yes," I whispered.

She was quiet for a minute and, to me, it felt like time had stopped. I was caught between so many things—wanting to get Dr. Wentworth or shake sense into Nan or soak up every last second with her.

"Well, if it's to be today," she said finally, "so be it. I'm ready."

I started to cry. The tears came so suddenly and violently that I couldn't keep up with them. They ran down my cheeks, gray trails of salt and mascara. "But I'm not," I squeezed out.

"Come here, Cassie."

I walked to her side, too agitated to sit on my pillowed chair. She stretched out her arms and I leaned in, resting my head on her shoulder. She stroked my hair.

"I know, honey. People rarely are. But it's going to happen someday. If not today, tomorrow. If not tomorrow, next week." I felt her head shake and knew I'd see her crooked grin if I looked up. And if I could see through my tears. "Why people think they can postpone the inevitable is beyond me."

"But, Nan, maybe we can. Postpone it, I mean." I had pulled away and was watching her. "Are you really ready to die?" I flinched at my own bluntness, but Nan didn't.

She was silent, looking into my eyes. I'm not sure what she was searching for, or whether she saw it, but she smiled and brought her hand, soft like a worn paper bag, to my face, erasing tear tracks. "Remember what I said about your mother? Was I glad that she died? Never. But was my life better because of it? Not because she wasn't in it, but because you were? Immeasurably. Maybe today is my day to go so that you can move on to what's next. The better things ahead for you in life."

"Forget it, Nan," I said. "That's baloney." How could she even say that? "How is being an orphan—not just without parents, but without *anyone*—going to make life better?"

I thought I saw the sparkle of a tear. "I'm sorry, Cassie. It will be hard, you're right. But you're a tough cookie."

I didn't answer.

"As Tasha would say, 'Suck it up.'"

"I don't want to suck it up, Nan. I want to do something about it."

"Well, I don't, Cass. Think about it. Really think. If this is our last day together, do you want to spend it running around after Dr. Wentworth? Having them do test after test, pull blood work, send me in for CAT scans and God knows what else?"

"I don't know, if it means it might not be the last day. . . ."

"But what if there's no changing things? You're going to call me crazy, but in a way, it's a gift to know that we may only have a little time left. At least we can choose how to use it."

I didn't agree with her, but I didn't know what to do next. Dr. Wentworth was a brick wall. I mean, there had to be other tests they could run, but at sixteen with a morbid hatred of biology, I had no clue what. Nan was watching me. I knew the look on her face. The one she wore when she saw me struggling with a problem that she knew the right answer to, hoping I would choose correctly. I closed my eyes and took a deep breath, exhaling slowly. I didn't want to look back in a year or five or ten and know that I had made Nan's last hours miserable. Especially when the mark might be useless. I took another breath, held, exhaled, and tried to let go of everything: worries about tomorrow, about a future without Nan, about how today would end. I focused on the only thing that mattered. I opened my eyes to see her still watching me.

I pulled my chair close, sinking into the pillows piled high on top, and took her hand. It was birdlike in its lightness, but still surprisingly strong. "I love you, Nan."

She smiled then, the creases at the corners of her eyes folding onto one another, well practiced in the art of joy. "Thank you, Cassie. I love you too."

We talked. Of things and nothings. School, my mother, the apartment, Nan's ex-husband, bits of her childhood in an ethnic neighborhood—Greektown, she called it. The day drew on, grew darker, and, though the misty light around her never faded, I started to hope. Dr. Wentworth stopped back, surprising me. We sent him away. Tina came in and out, leaving Nan with a kiss on her final visit, black cloth coat and purse in hand.

"I'll see you tomorrow, Nan," she said.

Nan smiled. "Good night, Tina. Thank you for everything."

Tina smiled back, but her mouth twitched, a trace of sadness, as she turned to leave.

Dinner was delivered and cleaned up. Eight passed, then nine, then ten. Nan nodded off, but I stayed there, holding her hand, watching the clock, hope slowly, cautiously growing.

And then, against all odds and plans, I fell asleep. I was exhausted. I could feel it, but I had counted on anxiety and adrenaline to keep me awake. And it had, but with Nan breathing softly and a TV droning in a room nearby, I felt my lids drooping. I remember thinking I could rest my head for just a minute.

As soon as I woke up, I knew she was gone. I could feel the cold in her hand. My face was wet before I even raised it from the bed where it had fallen. She was calm, her face serene and pale and statuesque in a way that made it clear that Nan, my vibrant, strong, loving, solid Nan, was gone. And so too was the light.

chapter 5

Agnes's nephew John drove us to the funeral. I sat in the back-seat, a thousand miles away, clutching a sleeve of tissues. My head felt wrapped in cotton. I could barely hear Agnes's sobbing or John's attempts at conversation.

The sun was unnaturally bright, glinting off the metal of car after car lining the neat lanes and perfect grass of the cemetery. The pain of its sharp glare hardly registered as I stared at the people, so many of them clustered around that awful hole. I recognized Nan's charity friends, her yoga partners, neighbors, a ton of old people I knew vaguely or not at all. Tina and Dr. Wentworth were there too. I could feel Tina's eyes on me, but I didn't look at her. We had already spoken the day after Nan died.

I had been sitting in a hallway at the hospital, filling out endless, incomprehensible paperwork, when I saw motion at the periphery of my vision—Tina, probably making the sign of the cross. I could tell from the look on her face that she was scared.

"Cassie," she whispered, coming hesitantly toward me. "I am so, so sorry."

I shrugged. "I guess it was her time."

She didn't say anything, just looked at me, her eyes deep brown pools, bottomless. I went back to my forms, angrily wiping the tears that had started again.

"You knew."

She said it so softly that I pretended not to hear.

"Cassie." This time she waited for me to meet her eyes. I finished filling in our address for the sixteenth time on the fourteenth form before looking up.

"What?"

"How did you know?"

"It was just a feeling, Tina." I ducked back into the papers again, ignoring her. She didn't want to listen when it mattered, and I'd be damned if I'd waste my time on her now.

"But . . . you were so sure." When I didn't answer, she said, "I'm sorry we didn't listen. Do more. Help."

"Nothing you could have done."

She'd thought about asking more. I could tell from the way she lingered, but in the end she said only, "Take care of yourself, Cassie."

Dr. Wentworth had been less curious. In fact, acted as if our dialog the day before had never happened. "No way to predict or prevent, I'm afraid. A stroke like that can happen to anyone. Just a coincidence that she was even at the hospital."

I stared past them when they offered condolences after the burial. Dr. Wentworth pressed my hand between his and murmured stock phrases. I'm not even sure Tina spoke, her dark eyes still bewildered.

People from school came too: classmates, teachers, Principal McCarthy. Tasha told me they'd let kids leave early, which explained why I suddenly had so many friends. That's too cynical, though, because the people I had the heart to talk to honestly seemed sympathetic. More than I could bear. "Thank you for coming," I told them and everyone else who filed past me and the brown box where Nan lay.

I had expected those first few days to be the worst—the hospital, the funeral, going back to our apartment—but it was after, when the people and the decisions and the questions receded, when everyone else's life took on its normal rattle and hum and I was left with quiet and solitude in mine, that it became unbearable.

I can't even say what I did those days after the funeral, when Nan was really, truly gone. There were times I'd realize only as I was getting ready for bed that I'd forgotten to eat. Other days I didn't need to put pajamas on, having never made it out of them.

People tried to fill the void. Tasha's parents had me over for dinner as often as I'd come. Agnes dropped by afternoons. She was withered by Nan's passing and I usually ended up comforting her, passing her tissues or brewing tea "just like Nan's," she would say, sprouting fresh tears.

It seemed weird to me that I was there on my own at sixteen. But with no family, where else could I go? Nan's lawyer had asked if I needed someone right away, while they sorted out her affairs. I didn't. There were people I could call if I had to. Still, it was strange to be so alone and I started to hate it in the apartment, those five rooms that used to feel warm and secure.

To escape their stillness, I ventured out more. Back on the bus, staring, but rarely seeing the scenery slide by. I walked the streets of Ashville, past all my favorite spots: the bookstore, Juan's newsstand, the square. There was no joy in it, no sense of adventure. I had to force each step and watched footfall after footfall. Not ready to face what I might see on the passing people if I looked up.

I took one of the sleeping pills someone had given me when I got home each night and sometimes another when I woke up.

When they were almost gone, I figured I might as well go back to school.

I'd been afraid being there would be uncomfortable, but Ashville isn't a big place. I'd known my classmates pretty much my whole life. We might not be close, but I was there when Lucy Donato's mom had cancer and Albert Lee's dog was put down and when Jolanta Harris broke her leg. Not literally there, on the scene, but in the hallways and classrooms, sitting near them, helping them pretend life could go on until they didn't have to pretend anymore. We knew how to treat one another in times like this. Going back to school *did* suck, but not because anyone said or did the wrong thing. Just because life in general sucked right now.

Tasha was my self-appointed guardian, walking to classes with me, at my locker during breaks. She seemed to get it that it was okay to be *near* people, but that I didn't really want to talk. Or look at them, if I could help it. There were times, though, that she was at doctors' appointments or classes and practices that didn't mesh with my schedule. It was during one of these that Jack Petroski found me.

"Cassie!" He broke away from his baseball teammates and trotted over. Final bell had just rung and I was collecting books from my locker slowly, not relishing my solitary trip home to the empty apartment. "Hey," he said softly, standing tall and slightly awkward at my side. "I wanted to say how sorry I am about Nan."

"Thanks, Jack." I glanced at him, saw genuine concern in his eyes, and looked quickly away.

"How are you?"

I shrugged and pushed hard against my locker to secure its bent latch. "Surviving."

He nodded and seemed about to go, but then asked, "You heading home?"

"Uh-huh."

"Want company?"

"Don't you have practice?"

"Nah. Coach is at the dentist. Gave us the day off."

I shrugged again. Jack didn't live near me, but I didn't have the energy to argue. "Sure."

He hefted my book bag, carrying it easily along with his own. Jack was already tanned from hours of practice, and his hair, an earthy brown, lay wavy and rumpled as if he'd just run his hand through it, something he often did. I wondered briefly where Val was and if she'd be angry. Not that there was anything wrong with two friends talking. That's what we were. Friends. Or had been back when the day's big challenge was who could climb highest in the maple tree behind school.

"So, you guys ready for play-offs next week?" I asked as we went down the five wide steps out front. It felt weird to be asking about something so ordinary. Not bad, necessarily.

"Sure," he said. "LaSalle's got some great hitters, but I think we can take them."

"Your mom going?"

"Oh yeah. She'll be head-to-toe black and orange, and asking the whole time why our school colors couldn't be something more flattering."

"We all wonder that," I said, smiling. "I hear some of the colleges have been watching you."

He nodded, looking more serious. "I think one or two might actually come out for the games."

I looked up at him, surprised. "But . . . that's a good thing, right?"

"It is," Jack answered slowly. "I just want to, you know, enjoy the game. Have fun. The scouts make it . . . I don't know . . . too real."

"I can see that," I said, nodding. "Where are they from?"

"Granville and WSU. Both have great baseball programs."

"Mm-hmm." I'd never heard of either, which meant absolutely nothing. The only thing I knew about baseball was that our team was really good and it was mostly because of Jack, the star pitcher. He'd started varsity as a freshman last year and even made the paper a few times. "And, uh, where exactly are they?"

"Granville's in Texas and WSU's in Kansas."

"Wow. Far."

"Not too many worthwhile programs around here, so I won't have much choice." Jack hitched his shoulder, adjusting our bags, then looked down at me. "How 'bout you?"

"Nah," I said. "No one's recruited me yet."

Jack grinned, nudging my arm with his. "You know what I mean. Have you started thinking about schools?"

"A little. Maybe Galein."

He nodded. "Great school. You visited yet?"

"No. Still waiting for their packet." Before Nan's death, I had scanned the mail every day for their letterhead. I was surprised to realize I'd actually forgotten to check for a day or so, couldn't remember the last stuff we'd—I'd—gotten. For all I knew, it was patiently waiting in our little keyed box.

"Where else are you going to look?" Jack asked.

"I don't know. I was thinking maybe Richford and State. I didn't want to go too far away." I shrugged. "Though, now, I'm not so sure . . ."

He nodded slowly. "I guess a lot seems different for you now. It'll still be nice to be close to here, though. Your friends and stuff."

"Yeah." I didn't bother pointing out that when everyone left for school, there wouldn't be anything or anyone here.

We were halfway to the apartment already. It was such a relief to have a normal conversation like this—about school, the future. I don't think I'd had one with anyone, even Tasha, since Nan had died more than two weeks before. I sighed. Jack looked down at me and, seeing it wasn't a sad sound, smiled.

"You know what I found the other day?" he asked.

"What?"

"Mickey Mouse poker chips."

"You did not."

"I did. I was looking for a picture of the fourth-grade baseball team for some project the cheerleaders are doing and it was there, in that box."

Jack's uncle Ray had taught us to play poker when we were eight. Before Jack and his mom moved to their new townhouse, they'd lived three blocks from me and Nan. After school, Ray would come over, done with his mail route by two, and we'd play. Penny ante, two-penny raises. For Christmas that year, he gave us each our own chips. Jack got Mickey, I got Minnie.

I smiled. "I'd forgotten all about those. I wonder what happened to my set. I'm sure I kept it."

Uncle Ray died just after my tenth birthday. The first funeral I'd ever gone to. Jack had cried and that scared me.

"He was a good man," I said.

"Well, I don't know about that." Jack smiled. "But he was a lot of fun." We crossed the street, both of us slowing as we turned onto my block. "So, you're staying in the apartment?" he asked. "Just you?"

"Where else would I go?"

"Right, I know, but isn't it . . . lonely?"

We had stopped at the concrete path that led into my building. I looked up and saw the yellow curtains of Nan's bedroom, still and dark. I kept that door firmly closed. Not ready to go there yet. I remembered early last spring, coming home on a bitterly cold day to find the apartment filled with daffodils, the same hue, but five shades brighter than Nan's curtains. She'd needed some sunshine, she said.

"Yeah," I answered Jack. "It is."

It had been a nice walk and I didn't want to end it like this. I started for the door, but he knew I was crying and stopped me, pulling me close, his sweatshirt warm and smelling faintly of sweat and aftershave. It felt so nice to have someone, maybe him especially, care that way: not protective like Tasha or commiserating like Agnes, but just caring. It broke open my sadness, tears wetting the navy cotton of his shirt.

He stroked my hair, waiting. Not trying to placate so he could leave. Just soothing, letting me be the one to pull away.

"I gotta go," I whispered, using the heel of my hand to wipe away tears.

Jack nodded. "If you need anything, Cass, you can come to me." His voice was low and earnest. "I mean it."

"Thanks, Jack," I said, because I knew he did.

Slowly I walked the long flight of stairs to the apartment. I thought about watching Jack from the window, wondered if he lingered outside for a minute or two, maybe thinking about coming up. Ringing the buzzer three times quick and once long and then bounding up the stairs, his legs taking the flight in four or five steps like he used to. I would have liked to see him, not a gangly kid anymore, someone much more grown-up, walking from my home to his, that link still between us. But watching him would have meant going into Nan's room.

chapter 6

"Are we next?"

I nodded, pulling the cord to let the bus driver know we wanted off.

"You know where his office is?" Tasha asked as we stood. We were holding the poles, but still stumbled like little kids when the bus lurched forward.

"No, but I've got the address. It won't be hard to find."

We were on our way to see Nan's lawyer, Mr. Koumaras. Tasha wasn't going in with me, but had offered to come along and wait out front. "I'll check out the business dudes," she'd said, winking as if they'd actually be worth checking out. "We'll hit Serendipity and The Brown Bean when you're done."

I agreed, hoping I'd be in the mood for shopping and coffee. I hadn't been on any of my other recent trips downtown. Having Tash along would probably help, but going through Nan's will—which is what I was here for—probably wouldn't.

Mr. Koumaras had called the day after Nan died, when I'd just come back from the hospital, my head feeling as puffy as my eyes looked. I'd registered snatches of the conversation, only remembering to show up at his office today because he left a message reminding me.

"So, tell me the rest," Tasha said as we started down Cedar Street. "What'd you talk about?"

"Oh, you know, nothing really. Colleges, the play-offs. You were right, scouts are coming to watch."

"Toldja," she said, smiling. Tasha made it her business to fill me in on all gossip about Jack, not that I'd ever asked her to or encouraged it. She had a thing about him and me. It had started about a month after she came to Ashville in eighth grade. We were at my locker and he'd stopped to ask me something. Tasha was smirking when he walked away.

"What?" I demanded.

"You belong together," she said.

"What? Who?" I looked around.

"Don't play innocent, Cassie," she said, still smiling. "You and that guy Jack."

"What are you talking about, Tash? You're crazy. He has a girlfriend." He and Val had started going out that summer. So I'd heard.

She shrugged. "He may have a girlfriend, but he also has a crush on you."

"Come on," I said, careful to hide my eyes. I hadn't known Tasha very long back then, but had already figured out that she was good at reading people. Too good. "We're just friends. I've known him forever—we used to hang out when we were kids."

"Whatever," she said. "But don't tell me you don't think he's hot. Or that you don't have maybe the teeny-tiniest little crush on him too."

"You're crazy."

Of course, she'd ignored me and persisted in bringing him up randomly and not-so-subtly raising her eyebrows or winking at me when he passed. It was more funny than annoying—because Tash is a goof—and had become a running joke. Naturally, I'd told her about him walking me home the day before.

"So, that's it?" she asked as we crossed the street, almost getting run over by a pack of skaters.

"What else did you expect?"

"I don't know, did he try to kiss you or anything?"

"Tasha! You're ridiculous." I ticked off my fingers as I listed: "He has a girlfriend, he and I are just friends, we'd been talking about Nan . . ."

"Ah, you didn't tell me that part."

"Yeah . . ." I didn't want to get into what had happened. I'd replayed it all afternoon, alone in the apartment. That moment with Jack—being so close to him—hadn't really felt like a joke. It felt special, intimate, and too fragile to share. "Anyway," I said, keeping my tone light and glancing again at the address in my hand. "It was nothing. But I knew you'd want to file it away in your bizarro Cassie and Jack collection."

"You betcha," Tasha said, grinning. "Mark my words, Cassie . . ."

"Yeah, yeah." I waved dismissively, squinting up at the faded numbers on the building, the small happiness of the conversation deflating. "I think this is it."

"You sure you don't want me to come in with you?" she asked.

I shook my head, though I really wasn't sure at all. "That's okay. Hopefully I won't be long."

Tasha dropped her bag and sat on the lowest step while I ascended, my stomach in knots.

I must have looked shell-shocked when I came out an hour later.

"You'll never believe . . ." Tasha said, stopping when she looked up at me. "Cassie? What's wrong?"

I'd expected my meeting with Mr. Koumaras to be like the court dramas Nan had liked. A dry recitation of heretofores and aforementioneds. It had started out like that—sound mind and body, on this date of blah, blah, blah, a listing of assets. I was her sole beneficiary.

"Quite a nice sum she's left you," Mr. Koumaras commented, meeting my eyes for a reaction. "Four hundred eighty-two thousand dollars."

Almost half a million dollars. I'd long suspected Nan had money socked away, though I would never have guessed such a ridiculous amount. Someday I'd probably be excited about it. Right now, I was just glad it was enough that I didn't have to think about it.

And then he'd dropped the bombshell: the guardianship.

"The what?" Tasha said as we sat on the steps out front.

"I know," I said, my head down, fighting tears. "That's what I said."

It was temporary, Mr. Koumaras explained. Ninety days mandated by the will. The inheritance would be held until it was completed.

"I don't even care about the money," I told Tasha, still trying to sort it all out. "But without it, I don't have anything to live on. He was talking about bills and mortgage and insurance." I shook my head. "I hadn't really thought about that kind of stuff."

"Maybe that's why Nan did it."

"Yeah, I guess, but . . ."

"What?"

I was angry that Nan hadn't told me, but maybe it did make sense to have some help. "Okay," I'd said to Mr. Koumaras. "Let me talk to my friend Tasha. I bet her parents would do it. Or maybe Agnes . . ."

He held up a hand. "Nan already designated a guardian."

"Oh. Well, which is it?" Why hadn't Tasha's parents said anything when I'd been over for dinner? Or Agnes the gazillion times she'd sat weeping on the sofa?

"Neither." He looked at his papers. "Nan designated Andrea Soto."

"Who?"

He turned to another page and read, "Andrea Soto, Fifty-four Weston Avenue, apartment twelve, Bering, Kansas. Ms. Soto is the only sister of Daniel Renfield, Cassie's father. She is Cassie's only living relative."

My dead father's sister. Who I'd never met. That's when the tears started, stinging and hot at the corners of my eyes.

"I don't know her," I said, trying to keep my voice steady. "I didn't even know my father had a sister. Nan can't have meant for me to . . . what? Go live with her?" At that, I started crying for real, the idea of leaving my home to live with a total stranger just too much. "This lady is not going to take care of some girl she doesn't know from a hole in the wall. Nan never talked about this . . . this Andrea Soto. She probably has no idea I even exist."

"Oh, no, she knows," he said softly, shuffling more papers and trying to ignore my tears. "She knows and has agreed to take you in." He'd tapped the page, then placed it neatly at the edge of the desk, facing me.

"Oh my God," Tasha gasped as we sat on the steps outside the lawyer's awful mousehole of an office. "How soon do you have to go?"

"Next week," I said. "He said I could wait until school was out or whatever, but if I do, I'll miss the beginning of next year here. I'd have to start in Kansas." I wiped my eyes. "I figured I should just get it over with."

Mr. Koumaras had assured me there were no other strings and that I'd probably be granted emancipated minor status without much trouble, what with the inheritance. Turning seventeen soon after would help, but wasn't a requirement. We'd only have to prove I was able to take care of myself. "It's not so bad, is it, Cassandra?" he'd said.

Yeah, it's great, I thought. Nan is gone, I see almost-dead people, and I have to leave my home and friends to live with an aunt I never knew about for the summer. In Kansas of all places. Terrific. "No, not so bad, I guess," is what I'd said out loud, trying to smile, but failing miserably.

"But what about finals?" Tasha asked, looking shell-shocked now too.

"He'll take care of it. Call Principal McCarthy."

"But . . . why, Cassie?"

"Why what?"

"Why would Nan do it? Send you out there?"

"Who knows?" I shrugged tiredly. "But I don't have much choice, so it doesn't really matter."

"But you're going to miss the play-offs and Matt Glassman's party and—"

"Yeah, I know. Don't remind me."

"I'm sorry, Cassie."

"Me too." I took a deep breath, trying to think positive thoughts about the next three months. Nan had often said you can live with anything as long as it's temporary. I hoped she was right.

chapter 7

The girl next to me picked up a magazine, then a minute later put it down. Her pale forehead was glistening. She looked at her watch and sighed, the exhale of a person barely able to catch her breath.

"What time are we supposed to land?" she finally asked.

"Two twenty," I said.

She nodded curtly, gripping her armrests as the plane jostled.

"Are you scared of flying?" Dumb question, I thought. Is the sky blue?

She glanced at me and nodded briefly, her color blanching at another bump.

"There's nothing to worry about," I told her with total confidence. "The plane will land safely."

"Easy for you to say," she muttered.

In fact it was. A small comfort of the mark—the only one I'd found so far. "Really. It's going to be okay."

She looked at me hard, but I noticed her grip on the chair loosen, a slight flush of the knuckles. She smiled weakly. "You're very convincing."

I smiled back and returned to my book, but I was too anxious to read. Had been most of the flight.

Tasha and I had closed up the apartment the day before with promises from Agnes and her nephew to keep an eye on it while I was away.

"God, I can't believe you'll be gone the whole summer," Tasha'd said as we sat on the stoop out front. "What am I going to do without you? Who will be my coffee bud? Or go swimsuit shopping with me? You're the only one I can trust!"

"Yeah. It stinks," I'd said.

And it did. But after I'd gotten over the initial shock, I realized how hard the past weeks in Ashville had really been. I missed Nan so much. Reminders of her tugged at me endlessly, places we'd gone or talked about, things we'd done together.

It wasn't just that, though. It was the mark. I couldn't handle seeing it on someone else I knew. What if it were Juan at the newsstand or Agnes or Tasha or Jack Petroski? If I stayed, someday it could be. It was bad enough knowing it was someone's time, but I wasn't ready to face the added burden of knowing their history and dreams, the family they'd be leaving behind to feel the way I felt now.

I'd started to think it wouldn't be so bad to be with strangers for a little while.

"And what about play-offs, Cassie?" Tasha threw up her arms melodramatically. "You're going to miss your man's starring role!"

"You are such a nerd," I'd told her, smiling, though I'd had to force it a little, which was truly stupid because it wasn't like, if I'd stayed in Ashville, I'd be likely to see Jack much anyway. Or that it would amount to anything more than "Hi, howya doin', how's your summer?"

I hadn't gotten to say good-bye to him. I'd tried, but every time I saw him the past week, he'd been with Val or his teammates and I felt weird calling him away to tell him I was leaving.

I'd almost caught him two days ago as he'd run past me down the school steps. I called his name, amazed to see him finally alone.

He turned, giving me a big smile. "Hey, Cass! We're taking off for the first game. Wish me luck!"

"Good luck," I said, his back already turned as he jogged toward the waiting bus.

I decided I wasn't going to mope about Jack, who probably wouldn't even realize I was gone, much less care. And, though I knew I'd miss Tasha, I'd started to feel a tickle of excitement at the thought of a few months in Bering. A fresh start.

Now that the day was here, though, mostly I just felt sick to my stomach.

Andrea Soto was meeting me at the airport. "I'm average height, dark hair. I'll be carrying a big orange bag," she'd said in our brief phone conversation. "My work tote. It goes with me everywhere, probably the best thing to pick me out with."

I hadn't been sure what to expect when Mr. Koumaras told me she'd be calling. Would it be a teary reunion? Condolences about Nan? Would she talk about her brother, my father?

It turned out to be none of these, purely logistical: where we would meet, her phone number, address. Just the facts, ma'am. That was fine, I thought, after we'd hung up. The rest of that stuff would be better in person anyway.

At a patch of turbulence, my seatmate inhaled sharply and practically threw her magazine to the floor. "Stupid, I know," she said through clenched teeth. "Fear isn't always rational."

I liked that.

When the bumping and bouncing stopped, she turned to me. "Sorry to be such a nutcase."

"Not a problem."

"I'm Petra," she said. "I'd offer to shake, but my hands are sweaty."

I smiled. She had black hair, dyed and clipped in a sharp bob around an elfin face. She wore heavy eyeliner, heavier boots, and was reading something with lots of technical-looking charts that I couldn't decipher without being snoopy. She reminded me of Tasha somehow, though they looked nothing alike. "Interesting name," I said.

"Thanks." She waited before prompting, "And you are . . . ?"

"Sorry. Cassandra. People call me Cassie, Cass, take your pick." I had known it was my turn, but held back. I don't know why, really. What could be the harm in telling her my name? Except that it meant I knew someone, someone knew me. Connection. One thing I was hoping to leave behind.

"Beware of Greeks bearing gifts," Petra said, smirking.

"That's right." I was surprised. Despite the goth look, she was sharp. Not many people knew the history behind my name.

"You live in Wichita?" she asked.

"No. I'll be staying there for a few months. Not Wichita exactly," I corrected, "but a town called Bering."

She nodded. "I've been there. Nice place. I live in Ridgevale."

Seeing my blank look, she added, "It's about midway between Wichita and Bering." She waited for a reaction, but having never been west of Pittsburgh, I had none. "Do you have family there?"

"Uh-huh. My aunt." It felt weird to say it, even though I'd been tossing it around in my head since Mr. Koumaras had told me about her.

"Oh, yeah? What's she do in Bering?"

"I don't know."

Petra looked at me strangely. "How old is she?"

I shrugged. "Not sure. Maybe forty? Fifty?" Though she could just as easily be ten years older or younger. I hadn't thought to ask.

She frowned. "So . . . you're going to live with your aunt, but you don't know how old she is or what she does?"

"I've never met her."

She raised her eyebrows. "How come? Was she locked up somewhere? Or is it a family feud?"

I don't know why I'd been worried about being snoopy. Clearly this girl wasn't, but she was so openly curious, it was disarming.

"No," I answered. "I don't think so, at least. I just found out about her. I didn't know I had an aunt."

"Wow. So, it's like a long-lost relative thing? Like on soap operas?"

I smiled a little. "Yeah. I guess it kind of is."

"Cool," she said, her dark eyes gleaming. "What *do* you know about her?"

"Well . . ." I reached into a pocket to pull out a wrinkled paper. "I've got her address."

Petra looked at it. "Great neighborhood. About as hip as Bering gets."

That little spark of excitement was back. But then Petra added, "Which isn't very, by the way."

Oh. Well, this was Kansas, after all. What did I expect?

In fact, I'd looked it up after my meeting with Mr. Koumaras and expected exactly what the Chamber of Commerce Web site told me: the ninth-largest city in Kansas, top twenty for wheat production, farming the principal occupation. Bering is the home of Lennox University and a vibrant downtown scene.

Petra snorted when I said it. "Vibrant, my ass. Though it beats Ridgevale."

I was about to ask why she stayed if she didn't like it, when the nose of the plane dipped, the start of our descent. Petra gasped and clutched the armrests. We passed through the clouds— cotton candy dreamscapes—and on the other side, I got my first look at Kansas: a patchwork of fields—gold, amber, brown, and green—broken by strips of road with tiny cars and trucks inching along. It looked quiet and peaceful, unfamiliar, yet welcoming.

Once the wheels touched down, Petra relaxed and bent forward, rummaging in her bag. She thrust something at me.

"Here, this is my card." Black, of course, with clean white lettering: *Petra Gordon, PhD, Psychiatry*. Never would have guessed. Plus, she must be older than she looked. "I'd be happy to show you around, if you want. Check out the vibrant downtown scene and all."

"Thanks." I tucked it in the outer pocket of my worn backpack, knowing I wouldn't call. "So you're a psychiatrist?"

"Yeah. Surprising, isn't it?"

"Well . . ."

"Most people would believe I'm seeing a shrink before they'd believe I *am* one."

"It's not that. You just seem too young to be done with all that schooling and stuff."

She nodded. "Well, I'm actually not. Done, that is. I'm doing my residency in Ridgevale, so I am a psychiatrist, but not licensed to practice on my own yet."

"Uh-huh." That explained why Petra was here. And made her fear of flying even funnier.

"I don't really use those cards," she added. "Not professionally. A friend got them printed up for shits and giggles. They sometimes come in handy, though."

"Like when you meet clueless strangers on airplanes."

"Right," she said. "Something like that."

We had taxied to the terminal and I felt the slight jolt of plane meeting Jetway.

"Anyway," Petra said, collecting her bags. "Be sure to pick up the *City Paper*; they've got the best list of what's going on. You know, concerts, shows, street fairs, that sort of thing. Plus, it'll give you a good lay of the land. There's usually something happening at the U and even if there isn't, it's a pretty cool place to hang out."

"Great," I said as she scooted for the door. "Thanks for the tips."

She waved over her shoulder and was gone.

chapter 8

I picked Andrea Soto out of the crowd immediately. Partly because the crowd was only six people, three of them men, but mostly because she was yelling into her phone so loudly that it was impossible not to notice.

I sized her up while she was distracted. Andrea Soto was lean and muscled as if she did Pilates or yoga, with a big orange satchel slung over one shoulder, as advertised. She might have been pretty, except for the frown lines creasing her forehead, and she looked closer to forty than fifty, which, by my mental math, would have made her a younger sister to my father. Maybe a lot younger. He'd have been fifty-two now.

Andrea Soto glanced up, noticing for the first time the passengers trickling out the doorway from my flight.

"I gotta go," she told the person loudly. "No. No, you call *me* later." Her eyes scanned the crowd, still angry from the call, and any glimmer of excitement I'd felt seeing my new home from the air faded. I was within twenty feet of her when her gaze finally found me. Her expression didn't change.

"Hi." I smiled, my lips like Silly Putty across my face. "Andrea Soto?"

"Yeah." She glanced back at her phone, punching a button or two before dropping it into her bag and stepping forward. "You must be Cassandra."

"Cassie."

"Right. Okay, Cassie." She stuck out her hand, which I shook, feeling strangely like I was on a job interview though I'd never been on one and this woman was supposed to be my family. "Everyone calls me Drea." She pronounced it *dray-uh*, her voice husky like a smoker's. "You might as well too, I'm sure you don't think of me as your aunt any more than I do."

She looked at my bag, a small rolling suitcase I'd bought before the trip. "You have more stuff?"

"Uh-huh."

I trailed Drea to baggage claim, not unlike the four-year-old who struggled to keep up with Nan on our way to Miss Loretta's, though at least I knew Nan would've waited for me. This lady, I wasn't so sure. At the carousel, we stood mostly in silence watching luggage tumble onto the conveyor. I looked around, trying to keep my mind off the fact that I'd be spending the next three months with this sharp-faced woman who, at best, didn't seem to have time for me.

A lot of the people wore glazed expressions, on autopilot until they'd completed the motions to get from here to wherever they really wanted to be. For most, that would probably take a few hours. For me, much longer. Fleetingly I thought about calling Mr. Koumaras and telling him to forget it, I'd forfeit the money, but that was ridiculous, of course. Temporary, I kept telling myself. Three months. Ninety days. Less time than it takes to grow out a bad haircut, right?

It got better when we were in the car. A little bit.

"This your first time here?" Drea asked, her eyes flicking to the rearview mirror as she changed lanes.

"Umm..." I wasn't sure how to answer. Of course it wasn't my first time. Didn't she know I'd been born here? "My first that I remember," I finally said. I thought maybe she'd run with it, tell me about my family or, at least, about the town. When she didn't, I asked, "You grew up here?"

"Yeah. Couldn't wait to get out. Can't believe I'm back."

"How long have you been back?"

"Almost seven years." She shook her head, muttering, "Fucking incredible."

"Where were you before?"

"Atlanta. Went there for grad school and stayed."

So she hadn't been here when I was born. Or when my parents died two years later. I wanted to ask Drea more, but I worried that personal questions would sound like I was trying to get the scoop on what she could offer me this summer, rather than just being grateful she was taking me in. I assumed that's how she viewed it, though I didn't want to be here any more than she appeared to want me.

Of course, I had questions about my parents too. Plenty of them. But I could tell these would have to wait until another time. I let silence take over the car and she seemed fine with that.

Despite the awkwardness between us, there was something

immediately comfortable and familiar about the Kansas land-
scape outside. My window was partially open, smells of earth and
dried hay blowing gently through the car as we passed acres of
farmland, different from Pennsylvania's only in its flatness. It
looked like just the kind of place I needed right now—quiet, tranquil, and sparsely populated with people I didn't know.

It was two hours from the Wichita airport to Bering. Drea
and I talked a little more on the ride. I asked about her work, one
thing she seemed excited about, though it was hard to imagine
why. She went on and on about some promotion for a bank with
posters, flyers, contests, yadda, yadda, yadda. If I ever wanted to
talk, this was a sure-win category. For her, at least.

As we approached the city, the fields gave way to clapboard
farmhouses, less charming ranches, and the occasional strip mall.
When we passed a few mini-skyscrapers, I figured we'd arrived.

"This is my neighborhood," she said finally. "Bering East. My
apartment's just another block ahead."

I could see what Petra meant. Drea's neighborhood *was* kind
of hip. There were people out on their stoops, books in hand,
smoking cigarettes, and wearing all manner of clothes and shoes
and skin colors. The whole of the neighborhood looked about
four blocks long, with every nationality and lifestyle packed in.
Sophistication on a small-city scale. Perfect.

We lugged my suitcases up steep stairs to her apartment on
the top floor, the elevator broken. "Again!" Drea fumed.

The apartment was updated and airy, cozy and antique all at
the same time. I loved it.

"This'll be your room," Drea said after she'd led me down a
narrow hallway. "It's not much, but it's the best space I've got."

"Thanks," I answered. "It's awesome." And it was. Small, but one wall was totally brick, with a huge old-fashioned iron clock face. There was a woven straw carpet and Indian-print bedding in deep red and purple.

"Yeah," Drea said. "It's my guest room, but I'm not expecting anyone . . . well, anyone else . . . this summer." She slung my suitcase, the smaller one that she'd rolled in, onto the bed before turning back to me. "You know, Cassie, I work a lot. Nights, weekends. I travel, sometimes on short notice. My job is very demanding. You're welcome to stay here, but don't expect much from me. I won't be taking you to the mall or movies or . . . whatever it is, you know, kids like you like to do. You'll be pretty much on your own."

She left out "take it or leave it," but I got the picture. I thought it was time to let her know this wasn't my choice either.

"That fine," I said evenly. "You know, I would have been happy to stay in Ashville, but Nan's will said I had to come. I'm sorry to put you out like this."

She shrugged. "It's only for the summer, right?"

"Right." And then, because I couldn't fathom the answer, I asked her, "Why did you even agree to have me stay here? I mean, were you close to Nan or something?"

Drea shook her head. "Nope, barely knew her. I met her at the funeral." She dropped her eyes, the only uncertainty she'd shown all day. "Your father's funeral," she added, staring out the window. "Saw her a few other times. I'd actually kind of forgotten about her asking me to do this." Drea looked back at me, shrugging. "It was a long time ago. She was out here, caught me at a tough moment. I'd just divorced my husband, guess I was feeling a little lonely, vulnerable . . . maybe back then I'd been thinking about some kid left all alone, feeling that same way."

I nodded, not sure how to respond. The mention of my father

kind of threw me. It never left my mind that this was his sister, but she hadn't brought him up once until now. Before coming, I'd wondered if there would be weepy sessions over old photo books and stories about their childhood. The idea of it had filled me with an equal mix of curiosity and dread—I'd had enough of teary reminiscence from Agnes and Nan's other friends. But Drea clearly wasn't the type. Still, she was my blood relative, someone who knew the father I couldn't remember. It was jarring to be reminded of that and I wondered what I might learn about him and my mother over the course of these next ninety days.

Drea looked at her watch. "Listen," she said. "I hope you don't mind, but I should really get back to work. I've got a huge presentation tomorrow. I'm sorry to do this on your first day here . . ."

"No, no, that's fine," I said. "I'll just . . . you know, um, get unpacked and stuff."

"Great," Drea said, heading for the door. She stuck her head back in the room. "There's a set of keys for you by the front door. Feel free to go out or whatever."

"Thanks."

"Make yourself at home," she called, her heels click-clacking quickly down the worn floorboards. The door slammed shut behind her.

"I guess I don't have much choice," I said to the empty apartment.

chapter 9

I spent about an hour putting away my clothes and checking out the rest of the apartment. The only other rooms were the bathroom, which Drea had forgotten to show me, and her room, which I'm sure she hadn't forgotten but I wanted to see anyway.

I stood by the sofa looking out the big windows to the busy street below, feeling more energized than I had in weeks. If Drea wasn't exaggerating—and my brief experience told me she wasn't—I would have this place to myself a lot of the time. It would be like having my own apartment, a cool one at that, in a new town, with fresh, unknown faces. Not bad. Maybe Nan had had the right idea after all.

I decided to head out, attaching the keys Drea left me to my ring that still carried the ones for our Ashville apartment, my bike lock, and some other randoms.

The streets of downtown Bering were clean and lined with mature trees and iron lampposts. It was small, comfortable, and naggingly familiar, but in a good way. I felt at home. It was more than Bering being like Ashville, I thought. This is where I was from. It occurred to me, not for the first time, that I was born among these people, maybe in the same hospital as some, our mothers sharing a room or a doctor.

I wandered for a while, then, thinking I'd take Petra's advice and pick up a *City Paper*, circled back to the bookstore below Drea's apartment. I sat on an iron bench outside and flipped open the newsprint magazine. Right away I saw what Petra meant—there was a section dubiously titled "The Weekly Wassup," with lists of street fairs, outdoor concerts, poetry readings, a lot of them taking place right downtown or on the campus of Lennox University.

I'd circled a few that might be worth checking out, when three girls and a boy came out of the bookstore, smiling and laughing. They wore short-sleeved shirts and tank tops a little too early and reminded me of my classmates, even myself before Nan died, enjoying the final days of school. They sauntered down the street and, having already gone through most of the *City Paper*, I tucked it into my book bag and followed them.

"... not as good as *The Dead Zone*," the boy was saying as I fell into step a few paces behind.

"Or *Salem's Lot*. Or *Carrie*," a girl with short dark hair, nearly a crew cut, added.

"I never liked *Carrie*," a different girl, pretty with red hair, said.

"Maybe not the same caliber," Crew Cut agreed. "But what about *The Stand*?"

Yes, I thought. I wished I could join in. I'd add *Cujo* to the list. Maybe not the same caliber either, but I could never get the final scenes—the desperate mother, her dying child, the foaming dog—out of my mind.

"Anyway," the boy said, leading us around the corner, "it wasn't bad. Just not my fave."

"Well, I'll take it when you're done," the redhead said.

I followed them as they filed into a storefront coffee shop, its velvet drapes held back by thick brown ribbon. The rough wooden floor was covered with threadbare rugs in faded jewel tones. The smell inside, rich and spiced, was immediately calming, and without thinking, I breathed deeply, nearly closing my eyes.

"I love that coffee smell too." I caught just a glimpse of the man on his way out—dark-rimmed glasses, floppy hair, older than me: twenty maybe. Cute. In a buttoned-down shirt kind of way.

I smiled back and made my way to the counter.

Fifteen minutes later, I was snuggled in a well-used chair near the window, steaming coffee by my side. I felt good, I realized, better than I had in weeks. "If you don't like the view, change the scenery," Nan used to say. It wasn't that I thought I could escape the mark. I knew it would be back; it was only a matter of time. But if I saw it here, it would be on a stranger rather than someone I knew and cared about.

It wasn't that I missed Nan any less either, but the pain of her being gone wouldn't be as fresh if I didn't have to walk past the closed door of a room that had always been open. So much about Bering seemed right: my space in Drea's apartment, other kids debating my favorite books, and now my own little coffee shop.

I think then—before I'd even finished my first day in Bering—I decided it would be okay. Better than okay even: good for me. It was hard to imagine why Nan had sent me to live with

Drea—a woman she hadn't known very well, who didn't seem that interested in me, and who lived hundreds of miles from my home. Then again, maybe that was the point. Maybe Nan didn't really think I needed a caretaker as much as a place I could learn to take care of myself.

chapter 10

"Three large mochas and an iced raspberry smoothie," Doug called over the clatter of mugs and metal.

"Got it." I reached for the cups, still holding the Café American for the last order steady under the machine.

It was a lot less relaxing on this side of the counter, but I loved working at Cuppa, amid the organic smells of coffee and teas and surrounded by a steady hum of conversation.

I'd been in town just under a week when I decided to apply, after I'd explored all Bering's neighborhoods and lounged for hours, reading in the apartment and at Lennox—the U, everyone called it. There's only so much of that you can do, though. I got bored and found myself thinking too much about stuff I didn't want to. Plus, I didn't have a whole lot of money, my allowance held by Drea, who'd spent less than two hours with me since I'd arrived. She was always in a rush, sprinting to the shower, kitchen, and out the door every morning. Sometimes I never even saw her, just found a scrawled note on the table: "Sorry, AM mtg!" or

"Will be late tonight." She hadn't been kidding about being on my own, so I figured I'd better find something to do.

Doug, at the coffee shop, had been hesitant to hire me. His face fell as he scanned my application: the absence of previous employment, my temporary stay here.

"You've never worked before?" he asked.

"I've done volunteer work."

"Like what?"

"Well, soup kitchens, taking food to shut-ins, umm . . ." I tried to remember all the places I'd tagged along with Nan. I felt guilty sitting there with him watching me skeptically.

Doug nodded, looking a little more encouraged, but then frowning at my address. "You just moved here?"

"Yes."

"For . . . school?"

"No."

"Family?"

"Sort of."

He waited, but I didn't feel like getting into it. "And you're only staying for the summer."

"Uh-huh."

He nodded, his face grim. I could tell he was about to end our interview, and not the right way. I realized then how much I wanted the job. Not only for the money, but more so that I'd really have a place here. Belong. I took a quick breath and decided to go for it.

"Listen, I'll give it to you straight. The truth is I was living with my grandmother in Pennsylvania and she died about a month ago. My parents are gone, so I'm living with my aunt for the summer. I know it's not long, but maybe I can fill in for . . . I don't know . . . some of the college kids who work here during the year?" It was a guess, but it must have been a good one, because Doug's face relaxed a little. I pressed on. "I've come to this coffee shop every day I've been in Bering."

He nodded. "I know."

"I'd really like to work here. I'm a quick study and I won't take off on you."

Doug was young—early twenties at the oldest—with shaggy hair the color of a Kansas wheat field and deep brown eyes. He looked at me closely for a minute, just to make sure I wasn't bullshitting him. "I'm sorry about your grandmother."

"Thanks."

"You know, this job doesn't pay a lot. If you're counting on it for expenses or something . . ."

I shook my head. "I've got some savings."

He took another look at my sorry application and I held my breath until he met my eyes again. "Okay, Cassandra . . ."

"Cassie."

He smiled. "Okay, Cassie." He stuck out his hand and I shook it, his skin warm as if he'd just set down a pot of java. "If you want it, it's yours." He went over the details then. It wasn't much money, he was right, but it was enough to help with groceries and what-not and, more importantly, it gave me somewhere to go every day. A purpose.

It had been less than a week, but I was pretty sure Doug wasn't sorry he'd taken a chance on me.

I handed the Café American to the lady across the counter, scooped raspberries and ice into the blender, and started on Doug's three mochas. It was still an hour before the lunch rush, but we had steady traffic anyway. People began their mornings at all different times, I'd learned. First in were the businesspeople with newspapers under their arms, cell phones affixed to their ears, and barely a glance at me as they whisked their insulated cups away. The next wave ran from about seven to eight. Middle management, Doug called them. Like the businesspeople, but with older suits. They looked less stressed, but somehow more harried, like they couldn't ever remember where they'd left their wallet or car keys. The assistants and retail people were next, taking us up to ten o'clock. After that it was mostly college kids who'd stuck around for the summer and randoms—taxi drivers and graphic artists and mothers—groups on no set schedule, breaking up the waves of suits and sweats.

I jammed out the three mochas without looking up, thankful Doug hadn't called another order on top of this. Mochas and a smoothie were the kind of stuff that could really put you behind. I poured the pureed fruit into a cup, made a perfect whipped cream swirl, and expertly picked up the other three cups with my remaining fingers, setting all four on the bar together.

"Couldn't get enough of that coffee smell, eh?"

The floppy hair was slicked back and he wore a T-shirt instead of a button-down, but those green eyes behind dark-framed glasses were instantly familiar. It took me less than a second to place him. The guy I'd passed on my way in the first time I'd come to Cuppa.

"Well, I figured if I was spending all my time here, they might as well pay me for it."

His smile was uneven, charmingly lopsided. "I think they're getting their money's worth."

The bells, hung on silver cords from our wooden door, jangled and I glanced over his shoulder, feeling my knees go weak. I don't know why I was so surprised. I'd been waiting for this since

Nan died, though I'm not sure I'd understood how bad it would really be. It was like I'd been standing at the edge of a cliff, thinking it was just a short drop. Until I started to fall.

The light around the woman walking slowly to the counter and smiling at her companion was too bright to be a reflection or sunlight or anything but the glow I knew only I could see.

"Are you okay?" The guy was looking at me closely, his eyes more intense.

"Fine," I answered, barely hearing my own voice.

"You don't look fine. You're very pale." He followed my gaze toward the door, but she had moved to the counter now. Not that he could see anything anyway. He turned back to me. "You should sit down."

I nodded. "Yeah. I will. My break's in a few minutes." Doug was talking to the woman, taking her order. She was utterly ordinary. Nan's age or a little younger, with gray-brown hair and a slight stoop. She was pale, but not exceptionally so, thin, but not in a way that suggested illness. The kind of person I'd never notice. Except that she had the mark. I realized he was still watching me, glasses guy, his fingers loosely wrapped around the cups I'd set on the counter. "Really," I said, forcing a smile, "I'm fine. Probably too much coffee."

A blond woman approached the counter. "Lucas? Need help with those?"

"Uh, sure." He passed her two of the drinks and picked up the other two. "You sure you're all right?" he asked, lingering. His eyes were magnetic, the green of dewy grass, with thick, dark lashes. If I hadn't been so distracted, I'd have been happy to look at them all day.

"Chamomile tea, light, and an espresso," Doug called.

"Fine," I said to Lucas. "I've got to go."

He nodded and followed the woman, petite and very pretty, back to a table where they joined another couple.

My mind raced and I stole glances at the two women while collecting the makings of their drinks. How would it happen? Car accident? A fall? A tumor? I watched her as I brewed tea. I couldn't help it. She leaned her cheek against her hand, elbow propped on the table, listening to her friend with a slight smile on lightly wrinkled lips. She wore no wedding ring and I wasn't sure if I was more relieved or saddened by the idea that she would leave no one behind. Not that I knew for sure. There could be children, a boyfriend, maybe even a husband and she'd forgotten her ring today. Of all days.

"Cassie?" Doug stood a foot away, watching me stir the tea aimlessly.

"I'm sorry," I said, shaking my head. "I, uh . . ."

"You okay?"

I nodded.

"We've got a little lull. Why don't you take five and let me finish this order?"

I glanced back at the woman, talking quietly, still surrounded by that soft light. "Yeah. If you don't mind, maybe I will."

The back room at Cuppa was cluttered with castoffs from the front. I slid into my favorite: an easy chair whose purple velvet had been worn away completely from the seat. I spent a lot of my breaks relaxing back here, but there was nothing restful about it now. It was almost worse than being faced with her. Out front, at least I had tasks. Here I had only the anxiety in my gut and a white cinder-block wall where I swear I could see images of Mr. McKenzie, Nan, the West Lakes Elementary kids flashing like a slide show. I felt like crying, but I wasn't sure if it was because I was sorry for the woman or if it was thinking about Nan and the last time I'd seen the mark or if it was the reminder that as hard as I tried to be normal, make friends, hold a job—no matter where I lived or what I did, this awful thing would always be with me.

I tried to do the breathing exercises from Nan's yoga video, inhaling deeply, holding, then releasing to a slow count. After a few minutes, I felt calmer and realized that mixed with all the bad feelings was a weird impulse to talk to the woman out there. It was the first time I'd seen the mark on a stranger and known, for certain, what it meant.

The wall clock clunked, the heavy ticking sound it makes when the minute hand passes twelve. I was startled to see I'd already been in the back nearly twenty minutes, well over my allotted ten-minute break. I stood, taking another deep breath before walking through the swinging door and back to the front room, still not sure what I would do, expecting that she'd already be gone.

But she wasn't. She was reaching for her purse, the glow soft and constant around her as she stood slowly, leaning a bit too long on the chair for support. I felt physically shaky, light-headed. Should I talk to her? What could I say?

I watched as she walked toward her friend, waiting patiently near the exit. They smiled at each other and her friend opened the door. I thought about calling to her or maybe following her out.

Instead, I only watched her leave, the sun framing her in the doorway, almost obscuring the other light as she went.

chapter 11

I found her obituary in the morning paper two days later. Heart attack. She'd been a social worker, divorced, mother of three, sixty-eight years old. I leaned back, the iron bench outside the bookstore hard against my spine, and thought about the ones I knew for sure—this woman, Mr. McKenzie, Nan, Mrs. Gettis, the West Lakes kids. I'd seen the mark on all of them and they'd died the same day, but there was no other connection. Nothing matched. The way they died didn't seem to matter, nor did anything about them—age, gender, their work, whether they had family or not. The only commonality was that they'd crossed my path. But nothing explained why I saw it. Of all people, why me?

That day, I made my first visit to the Bering Library. It was a sleek, modern building and, loyal as I was to the Ashville Library, where I'd spent countless hours, I had to admit this library won any comparison, hands-down. It was awesome.

I started with medical reference and moved on from there. Over the course of six hours, I must have browsed fifty books on health, spirituality, psychic and paranormal phenomena, even the Bible. Nothing. Not a single mention of a physical or mental condition that would explain the mark or any references to people with an ability to see death, much less a guide about what to do with it or—what I really wanted—how to make it stop. Deep down I knew I wouldn't find that, of course. It didn't seem like the kind of thing I could get treated for, take some antibiotics or start a vegan diet and magically be cured.

I felt so guilty, a black and heavy feeling, like it was my fault or that I should *do* something, but what could I have said to the woman at the coffee shop? How would knowing she was about to die, but not how, have helped?

I wished then, and so many times after, that Nan were around for me to talk to. I needed a confidant, but the people I knew here—Drea, Doug, my coworkers—were totally out of the question.

I'd talked to Tasha every day my first week in Bering, but our conversations were squeezed between school, work, parties, and her road-tripping to see the baseball team at States. I understood. End of year was hectic. By week two we'd moved on to texting, short bursts about mostly nothing: the swimsuit she'd bought, a hot guy she'd be working with over the summer. I thought about confiding in her, but I couldn't figure out how to explain why I hadn't before, and it never seemed the right time to bring up death anyway.

So I kept to myself and did my best to pretend the mark didn't exist, focusing instead on my job and Bering, which, every day, felt more like my new home rather than my parents' old one. I still thought of them a lot. Being here, I couldn't help it. If I'd wanted to, I could have found out exactly where their house had

been. There were probably records—old phone books or deeds in
City Hall. Or I could have asked Drea. Even though she hadn't
been here, she probably knew. Certainly I could have found out
where the fatal accident happened. But I liked Bering—my
Bering—too much. I didn't want to know if my favorite street corner was where my parents died. Or that they'd lived in ramshackle
Clinton rather than smart, urbane U Park, where I always pictured them.

Instead, I went to student art shows and shopping at thrift
stores advertised in *City Paper*. When I felt like it, I stayed out
late, reading at the park on Bering's south side or sitting through
poetry readings at the U, though I quickly realized they weren't
my thing. I felt grown-up here, on my own, and that part was cool.
A little lonely, but cool.

It was after my second—and last—poetry event that I noticed
the signs outside the registrar's office advertising the final day to
enroll in summer session. I stopped, struck by the idea, knowing
I needed more to do, more to think about. I could almost hear
Nan as I stood there, watching the posters flap in the light summer breeze. "What are you waiting for, Cassie?" she'd have said.
"Just do it."

And so I did. It wasn't how I'd planned to start, but that day I
signed up for my first college class.

chapter 12

They shuffled into the classroom, mostly in flip-flops and sweats, barely awake, though it was well past ten in the morning. I'd known from Cuppa to expect this. I had studied their habits and clothes. I wore Converse and the cutoff jean shorts I'd found at a store near the apartment.

I'd picked a seat near the back of the room, a theater-style auditorium, but small. Fifty-six seats. I'd counted while I was waiting. The classroom was empty when I arrived and I worried that I might be in the wrong place or, as a noncredit student, have missed some important communication about schedule change. Turns out I'm just a geek, sitting with notebook, pencil, and my *Introduction to Philosophy* text way too early. The truth is, I was excited about being a part of Lennox—a quasi–college student, rather than just hanging around campus.

I didn't know a thing about philosophy except the familiar names—Aristotle, Socrates, Plato. The ancient Greeks—our people, Nan would have said. If I wanted to keep my brain busy, philosophy seemed a good choice.

The room started to fill about five minutes before class, the other students barely looking at me, dragging themselves to the closest chair or talking with friends. They didn't look like they shared my enthusiasm and I wondered why they were even in this class. Probably not by choice.

Everyone quieted when the professor walked in, wearing a plaid jacket and white beard. Santa Claus in madras. He placed his books and papers on the desk and, without a word, turned to the chalkboard and wrote: WHO AM I?

The letters were bold, sharp white against green. I'd had lots of teachers start class by writing their name on the board. This was a little different.

"Who am I?" he said aloud, his voice carrying easily over the rows.

No one answered. The professor looked up, scanning us closely. I felt as if he were committing each of our faces to memory, though that was impossible with more than half the room's chairs filled.

"No one read the course description?" he said, surprised. "No one knows who I am?"

There were a few chuckles, but that was it. He nodded, not surprised and only mildly disappointed. I felt guilty, but not enough to be the first victim. It was obvious from his tone, his stance, the fact that this was Philosophy 101 that the answer was more than just "Professor McMillan."

"I assume none of you have taken a philosophy course before. Correct me if I'm wrong." No one spoke. He continued patiently, "This is a course that will require lively discussion. I expect a great deal of participation and preparation. If you cannot commit to that, you are in the wrong class and I expect your seat will be vacant next class."

I thought he might find a lot of vacant seats, but mine wouldn't be one of them.

"So," he said, scanning the crowd. "Let's try this again. Who am I?"

"Professor McMillan?" someone finally ventured.

"Yeesss," Professor McMillan said dramatically, spreading his hands to the class. "See? It's not so hard, is it?"

A few people shook their heads. Of course, none of them had spoken.

"But," he said as I, and everyone else in the room, knew he would. "*Who* is Professor McMillan?"

The door opened then and my breath caught as I recognized the man with dark-rimmed glasses who strolled in, arms laden with photocopies. "Ah," Professor McMillan said. "Our summer TA has arrived. Lucas, thank you for joining us."

"A pleasure, as always," he answered, taking a seat in the front corner.

"Who am I?" Professor McMillan continued, giving up on us, "It's one of the great questions of philosophy. What defines us? What makes us who we are? Can we even be defined?"

He paused, his eyes sweeping the silent crowd. "Know thyself, for in knowing thyself, you understand others. Of course," he added, "the great philosophers also believed true self-knowledge was impossible."

A few students exchanged confused looks. Professor McMillan saw, but didn't acknowledge them.

"The human spirit is complex. The closest we can come to

understanding ourselves is by examining our values, our talents, our beliefs. What makes us happy? This will answer 'Who am I?'"

He nodded to Lucas, who stood and began counting stacks of the papers he'd come in with.

"Then we can move on to 'Why am I here?'" Professor McMillan paused thoughtfully. "Heavy stuff, huh?"

There were a few relieved laughs. He was right—much heavier than I'd imagined. It made my head swim a little and I hadn't even cracked a book, but I felt a thrill at the thought of doing so. It sure beat the things my brain was occupied with now: the ingredients of a mocha latte or how to make a Super Buzz-Buzz Espresso. And, of course, the mark.

"This is Lucas; he's part of our undergraduate teaching assistant program and will be helping throughout the class." Lucas smiled and waved. "We'll review the syllabus when you each have a copy."

Lucas handed the agenda for our biweekly class down each aisle. He paused when he saw me, smiled, and nodded before continuing on. I listened as Professor McMillan talked through the class outline. Socrates, Plato, Aristotle, Locke, Hume, Descartes, Russell, Kierkegaard. "Everyone's favorite optimist." A few more chuckles.

He reviewed the required texts and our first assignment, to be completed in the next three days. At the end of class, Professor McMillan thanked us for participating. "I look forward to seeing you on Thursday," he concluded. "Those of you willing to read and engage, that is."

Students stood, stretched, waved to friends, left in groups. I was in no hurry to go, wanting to savor this, my first college class. I collected my book bag and notes slowly, letting other students file past.

"Hello, coffee girl."

He was close enough that I could smell his cologne, sharp and woodsy, hitting the back of my throat, slightly dizzying. Or maybe it's just that I knew it was him. Lucas. I'd seen him a few times at the coffee shop, but we'd only spoken once. The day I saw the mark. Still, every time, there was that eye contact. The attraction now was unmistakable and I felt my heart pounding so hard with him standing next to me that I was sure he could see it through my thin T-shirt.

"You can call me Cassie." I kept my gaze level, confident.

"Yes. Cassandra Renfield. Our one audit student. You don't see a lot of people slogging through philosophy just for the fun of it."

"Well, maybe I don't know what I got myself into."

"Maybe." He didn't seem to have anything else to say, so I started toward the door. He followed. "Do you have another class now?"

"No. This is the only one I'm taking."

"Can I buy you a cup of coffee?"

I turned to face him, sure he was making fun of my job. "Are you joking?"

"Well, I know you like it."

"Love it. But don't you have another class or something?"

"No, that's it for today."

I hesitated. I don't know why. I'd thought about Lucas, remembering his name, said by the pretty blonde the first day. "Are you allowed to . . . fraternize with students?"

He snorted. "It's just coffee, Cassandra. I'm not asking you back to my apartment."

I turned bright red, could feel my face on fire and looked away, hoping he wouldn't notice. Right. He was quiet and it was horribly awkward. I felt like he could read my every thought.

"Come on," he said finally, softer. "It's a beautiful day. We'll sit outside."

Café Lennox was a Parisian bistro wannabe: striped awnings, iron furniture, umbrellas. Lucas and I took a seat on the brick patio facing the quad.

"Tell me about yourself, Cassandra Renfield," he said, leaning back with a slight smile after we'd gotten our drinks.

"Well . . ." I stirred my black coffee, trying to decide how to start. "I've been living in Bering for about two weeks. Moved here from Pennsylvania. I work at a coffee shop."

"You don't say."

I smiled. "Um . . . I guess that's about it. Not too much to tell."

"Surely there's more than that. Do you have brothers or sisters?"

"No."

"Did you move here with your family?"

"No, just me."

"Just you? Why?"

"Why just me or why did I move here?"

"Both."

I shrugged, not wanting to get into it.

Lucas frowned. "Well, was it to come to Lennox?"

"No." I didn't want to tell him I hadn't graduated from high school yet, wasn't old enough to be a real college student.

"Uh-huh." Lucas's smile had faded. "You're not making this

very easy, you know. This is supposed to be a conversation, not twenty questions."

"I'm sorry. 'Tell me about yourself' sounded more like a command than the start of a conversation."

He stared at me, then raised an eyebrow, slightly bemused, slightly annoyed. "You're a prickly one, aren't you?"

I shrugged again, feeling sulky. This isn't how I wanted this to go.

I guess Lucas had the same thought, because he sighed and said, "How about we start over? I'll go first." He extended his hand across the table. It was firm and warm and made me a little tingly. "I'm Lucas Canton. I'm eighteen—nineteen in October—going into my sophomore year at Lennox. I'm from California, just outside LA. My family still lives there: Mom, Dad, and two sisters. I like good food, great books, coffee, squash, skiing, and challenging conversation." He smiled wryly.

"I guess you've come to the right place."

"I guess so. Your turn."

"Okay. I'm Cassandra Renfield. You already know how long I've been in Bering and where I'm from." I paused, knowing I had to tell him more or this conversation would be over. "I'm staying with my aunt for a while. I was living with my grandmother in Pennsylvania, but she died last month. My parents died when I was young. They're buried here."

"Wow." He leaned back, one hand fingering his coffee cup, the other absently pinching his full lower lip. "I'm sorry about your grandmother. That must have been hard."

"Yeah, well. I'm okay. But thanks."

I looked away, wishing in the silence that I hadn't brought all of that up. I could have just gone with "living with my aunt" rather than spilling the whole story. Especially the bit about my parents. For God's sake, why on earth had I told my philosophy TA who I'd just met about them?

"So how about your dislikes?" I asked abruptly.

"I'm sorry?" Lucas had been looking out across campus, but turned back to me and I felt a slow flush as his eyes met mine. He was even better looking than I'd remembered from Cuppa. He had perfect skin and a nose neither small nor large, with a little bend in the middle. He wasn't exceptionally tall, maybe five foot nine or ten, but fit and athletic and totally unlike my image of a philosophy student. But it was mostly those eyes. I could see now that the green was speckled with streaks of gold and amber. All in all, sitting across from Lucas made it hard to think.

"Your dislikes," I said, taking a sip of coffee. I felt stupid, like I was pumping him for information, but I had to lighten the mood after bringing up all my baggage. "You told me what you like. How about the other half?"

"My dislikes . . . ," he said, thinking. "Wait a minute. You first—your likes. Don't think you're getting off the hook here, Cassandra." He smiled and any heaviness lifted from our table.

We covered all the basic ground. Favorite foods, music, where we lived, what we thought of Bering. We had a lot in common, I thought. Certainly that's what I wanted to believe.

"You'll like Professor McMillan," he told me.

"I already do."

"You'll learn so much from him," he continued as if I hadn't spoken. "He's tough, but great at challenging you to think, to question everything. They're not all like that, the profs in the department. In fact, most of them aren't."

"No?"

He shook his head. "I don't think I'd have even applied for the TA program if it'd been someone else. Most of them want you to dissect Plato's or Aristotle's arguments to understand *their* moral system rather than using it to discover your own."

"Interesting." I wasn't sure I had a moral system. If I did, I hoped my new professor had the user's manual.

"Not at all what the philosophers intended," Lucas continued. "You'll see what I mean." He checked his watch. I knew from the clock in front of the library that we'd barely been there a half hour, just long enough for coffee. "Ready to head out?" he asked.

He paid the bill and I didn't argue. I'm not sure what I'd hoped for, but his breezy "see you later" left me disappointed. Had my conversation not been challenging enough or had our attraction been one-sided from the start?

The hell with Lucas Canton, I decided, walking back to the apartment and grinning at the feel of my backpack, full once again, slung familiarly over my left shoulder. He wasn't what I'd been looking for when I enrolled at Lennox anyway.

chapter 13

I was tucked into a corner of the sofa when Drea came in
around seven. The keys in the door startled me. I was used to
hearing them only vaguely through a sleep-fogged brain, her
arrival usually long after I'd gone to bed. We'd had exactly two
meals together since I'd moved in, one of them a breakfast, which
she'd spent looking at charts and bullet points for some presentation.

"Hey," she said, tossing her orange bag onto the table beside
the door.

"Hey," I echoed.

She went to the kitchen and poured herself a glass of wine. I
returned to my book, fully expecting her to disappear down
the hall to her bedroom.

Instead she came into the living room and flopped into the
chair between me and the window with an exhausted sigh.

I considered asking about her day, it would have been
the polite thing, but I was much more interested in Plato

than Pete's Potato Chips, the account I knew she'd been working on.

"What've you got your nose buried in?" Drea asked.

I flipped closed the cover of my *Intro to Philosophy* text, holding it up. She raised her eyebrows.

"A little light reading?"

I smiled. "Actually, I signed up for a class at the U. Not for credit or anything. Just for . . ." I stopped. I was going to say "for something to do," but I didn't want to imply that I was bored and she should be entertaining me. "Just to, you know, get ahead," I finished instead.

Drea stared at me wordlessly, then frowned and turned toward the window. I figured she was worried about the money. "It didn't cost a lot," I assured her. "I'm covering it with what I make at the coffee shop." I had no idea how much she was getting from Mr. Koumaras, if anything, and I'd been careful about not using up her stuff, eating at Cuppa whenever I could.

"Mmm-hmm," she said absently.

I waited, but when she didn't say anything more, I went back to Plato, remembering how much I preferred it when she was out.

"You know, your father taught there." Drea was still looking away, her voice drifting, disembodied.

A-ha. I closed my book. "I did," I answered. "Ancient history, right?"

She nodded, finally looking at me, then down at her half-empty glass. "He always liked that stuff. I remember him reading about castles and knights. Not picture books, but big, heavy things." She made a C with her thumb and forefinger to show me the thickness. "A lot of kids are into that, but Danny always wanted the real story. Not the make-believe."

Danny. The name ricocheted in my head, familiar and intimate. A real person, not the black-and-white photograph he'd always been to me.

She continued, "My parents were so proud when he got the professorship at Lennox. It was a big deal that he went to college—neither of them had—but to *work* at one? Teach?" She shook her head. "It was as if he'd been elected president or something."

"Were you close to him?"

"He was seven years older so we were always at kind of different places in our lives, but yeah"—Drea paused, nodding—"we were pretty close. He was a good brother."

This was the most I'd heard Drea talk. I didn't know if it was the wine or what, but I figured this was my chance to learn something about my parents. "Do you know how he . . . Danny . . . and my mother met?"

Drea looked at me as if my speaking his name sounded as strange as it felt, though I'm sure that was my imagination. "You don't know?"

"No. Nan didn't really talk about them."

"I guess not." I couldn't quite place her tone—bitter and wistful and amused all together. "They met when he was in Pennsylvania for a semester. She ran away from home and came back here with him."

"What do you mean, 'ran away from home'?"

Drea shrugged. "Just that. She was sixteen. I don't think her parents would have *let* her go."

"What?!"

"Wow," she said, a little softer. "You really didn't know, huh?"

I shook my head, trying to absorb what she'd said. I'd been

expecting to hear about mutual friends or a blind date even. Not this. Nothing like this.

"Yeah," Drea said, taking another sip and looking out the window again. "We didn't realize she was so young back then. Danny kept that to himself. Kept the whole thing to himself for a while. He was finishing his graduate work in Wichita, so she just moved into his apartment, was there for months before we knew about it."

"Wow." I tried to imagine Nan's reaction. Was this why she'd never talked about my mother?

"Was she . . ." I wasn't sure how to ask it. I mean, I knew what I'd think if someone at school ran off with a guy in his twenties, but back then? In the kind of tight-knit, old-fashioned community Greektown had always sounded like?

Drea read my mind. "Your mother was a good girl, Cassie. Much more than I ever was, that's for sure." She paused, refilling her glass from the bottle beside her chair. "She missed your grand-mother a lot. Talked about her all the time."

"So why'd she leave? I mean, if she was so into my father, couldn't she just have . . . I don't know, dated him long-distance or something?"

"Who knows?" Drea said. "The way Danny told it, there was some bad stuff back home that she had to get away from. He was 'rescuing' her." Drea said the last sentence with a bitterness that made it pretty clear what she'd thought of my mother. Or at least of "Danny" being with her.

"What kind of bad stuff?"

"A friend of hers died. Her best friend." She sipped her wine. "Your mother was there when it happened and kind of lost it."

"What?! Jeez . . ." I couldn't believe Nan had never told me this. Any of it. "How did the friend die?"

"Stung by a bee."

"Huh?"

"Some kind of allergic reaction. They were at your mom's house with your grandmother and this friend, Roberta—God only knows why I remember that—swelled up, stopped breathing." Drea paused thoughtfully. "I guess I can see it being pretty freaky, especially for a sixteen-year-old."

"Yeah." I pictured watching something like that happen to Tasha. Terrible. "But I still don't get why she ran away. I mean, Nan would have helped her . . ."

"Dunno." Drea shook her head. "Danny said the girl's family blamed your grandmother, was furious that she'd let them play hooky. Maybe that had something to do with it."

That sounded like Nan. I remembered plenty of "field trips," as she called them, on days I should have been in school. Sometimes the museum, often the beach.

Drea drained the last of her wine before adding, "Or maybe your mom just jumped at a chance to get out of that shithole she was living in." She glanced out the window again. "She talked about it like she missed it, but it always sounded a lot like this place to me."

Drea stood, slightly unsteady and obviously finished with the conversation. I suspected these weren't her first glasses of wine.

"Enjoy your book," she said, walking carefully to the kitchen for a bottled water, then down the hall to her bedroom.

chapter 14

It was our second week of classes, day twenty-three of my ninety with Drea—not that I was counting—when the heat wave finally broke. I'd always thought the middle of the country would have more of a dry heat—something about the absence of the ocean. I was wrong. The humidity in Bering was as bad as Ashville. Worse, since our apartment back there at least had air-conditioning.

But finally, I woke one morning to find the fan's breeze crisp and dry across my legs. It was Tuesday and I had an early shift at Cuppa, six to eleven, but the rest of the day was mine and I knew just where I'd go—the park on the south side of Bering, my favorite place to study.

I was eager to continue our assignment, Aristotle's Nichomachean Ethics. Philosophy was every bit as interesting as I'd hoped, Professor McMillan pacing the front of the classroom asking question after question, the Socratic method, I now knew. I'd found myself doing it too, to see if Aristotle was right that everything we do has the end goal of happiness. Why did I wear a black shirt? Because I had to work and coffee stains on my clothes make me self-conscious. Black shirt equals clean and confident. Happy. Why was I making an espresso? Because if I didn't the customer who'd ordered it would get angry. Then Doug might fire me; I'd have no job and be back to moping around the apartment, maybe with Drea there. Definitely less happy. How could my mother have run away at sixteen? That one I had no answer for. Inconceivable.

Still, I thought Aristotle might be on to something.

I looked forward to our Monday and Thursday sessions. The empty seats in our second class were fewer than I'd expected, though I understood why Professor McMillan had warned us. Philosophy was hard. It could take an hour to get through five pages and really understand them, unlike my classes at Ashville High, where I'd mostly had to memorize dates and facts. This was *thinking*.

I'd started to wonder if maybe it could help me sort out the mark, answer some of the questions my trip to the library hadn't.

Professor McMillan had said that Lucas would teach part of our next lesson and I was eager to see how he'd handle it. He hadn't asked me to coffee again, barely acknowledged me in classes. I was disappointed, but tried to focus on the lectures instead of the way his dark hair fell gracefully forward as he jotted notes in a black journal.

It was just before noon when I entered the park carrying my bag filled with pencils, textbooks, and lunch. I had barely gotten to spread my blanket on the grass by the pond when I saw the woman with the mark.

I felt the familiar queasiness mixed with a tiny touch of relief, like the way you hold your breath during a scary movie until the killer jumps out or you finally see what's behind the closet door. I'd expected it to show up again, though not so soon after the woman at Cuppa. It made me worry that maybe it was somehow feeding on itself, getting stronger.

This woman walked right toward me, the glow clearly visible even in the bright sunshine. For a minute I had a weird feeling she knew and was coming over to yell at me or ask for help, but she was smiling, blissfully unaware.

"Here, Ginger!" she called, and I realized she *was* walking toward me, to fetch the dog who'd run to the edge of the pond.

At the sound of her voice, the dog turned and started back up the slope, stopping by my blanket. She sniffed at its edges, probably still smelling of Nan's incense. I felt the woman beside me, watched her well-used sneakers gently prod the dog away.

"I'm sorry," she said warmly. "Ginger, no!"

"That's okay. I don't mind." My voice was thin, barely able to force out the words. I looked up at her, shielding my eyes from the sun. Wishing I could cover them to block out the light around her.

"What a beautiful day," she breathed. She was older, maybe in her late forties or early fifties, slightly overweight and smiling. I could tell from the creases by her eyes and mouth that it was an expression she wore often.

"Yeah, it is," I said. Together we watched the pond, light glinting off soft ripples in the water like shiny fish flicking to the surface. Ginger had finished her inspection of my blanket, deemed it good, and moved on to my leg.

"Just push her aside," the woman said, shaking her head ruefully. "She can be such a pain."

"I don't mind, really," I told her. "I love dogs." I scratched

Ginger's ears, happy for the distraction. Her fur was warm and silky, and she rolled her head back, pushing into my hand for more. I stole another look at the woman, watching her dog fondly. Out of habit, I checked her left hand. No ring.

"I feel blessed to have days like these," she said. "I took today off for her vet appointment this morning. It's been so hot, I thought we'd end up inside most of the day, and look what we got instead." She turned her face up to the sky, still smiling.

I wondered, as I always did when I saw them, how it would happen. And whether it was better or worse that it was unexpected, as her death clearly would be.

Ginger looked up then, her ears perking at a squirrel scavenging nearby. Like a rocket, she was gone, blazing a path toward the nut tree the squirrel scampered up.

"Ginger!" The woman turned to follow, giving me a quick wave before she left. "Enjoy the day!"

"You too," I said automatically to her retreating back, immediately feeling stupid. Of course she wouldn't. I watched the woman standing by the tree, arms folded as she patiently waited for Ginger, running rings around the trunk. Finally the dog came to a stop, jumping up, scratching at the thick bark, before loping over to her master. The woman squatted, nuzzling the dog's neck and talking, the hum of her voice barely audible. I felt terribly sad. Why her? Why did she have to take today off work?

It was wearing on me, seeing these people with the mark. Knowing what it meant made all the difference, even though I tried hard to pretend it didn't. I mean, everyone dies, right? What did it matter if it was today or tomorrow or next year, or if I knew about it or didn't?

But it did matter. Even if I couldn't help, I had started to wonder if I was wrong not to tell them. Was I denying them a chance to make whatever final preparations there were: say good-bye, call their lawyer, or the mother or daughter they hadn't talked to all month, the husband they'd had a fight with last night? Or was it better to let things take their course, let that woman enjoy what she could of her last day?

I was so torn, my insides twisting at the idea of trying to tell her, not knowing how or if I really should.

The woman and Ginger lingered by a bench, then a trash can, then a bush. I walked to the edge of the pond. Closer, the flashes of light on the water were brighter, almost painfully so, sharp pin-pricks cutting across my vision. I closed my eyes, breathing deeply, willing her away. Letting indecision be my decision, like I had with the woman at the coffee shop.

When I finally went back to my blanket, she was gone.

And I felt awful.

chapter 15

"Today we're going to talk about right and wrong."

That was how Lucas introduced his lesson. Back home, it would have been "Tell me the first line of the Gettysburg address." Here it was life and death, good and bad, the meaning of existence.

"Ethics is the study of right and wrong, derived from the Greek word *ethos*, or habit," he said. "We are what we repeatedly do. Anyone ever heard that before?"

A few nods.

"It's one of my dad's favorite sayings," Lucas said. "I always hated it."

A few laughs. Already I could tell he was good and definitely more fun to watch than my teachers in Ashville. I'd been surprised Lucas would actually be teaching classes, but he was hardly on his own, with Professor McMillan right there watching and taking notes.

Lucas recapped some of the philosophies we'd covered: Plato's three souls—that "right" was when the mind, will, and desire were all working for the same goal—and Aristotle's "choice-worthy" actions, ones that avoided extremes. He moved on to Kant, who was beyond confusing. I'd had to search the Internet to learn that he thought you should do your duty, no matter what.

I'd spent a lot of time on this week's readings after seeing that woman in the park with her dog.

I hadn't looked her up. Didn't want to read about how her life had ended and who she'd left behind or hadn't. I was sure she'd died—no longer needed the black-and-white confirmation—but I couldn't stop thinking about whether I'd done the right thing.

At the front of the room, Lucas kept talking, but I wasn't really listening to him, unable to ignore the question that had been less than a whisper when Nan died, but grew louder, more insistent, each time I saw the mark. Should I tell or not?

I'd scoured the philosophy readings, but it wasn't there. None of them ever got down to how to tackle a real problem, one with lots more gray than black and white. I'd hoped for more. I wanted answers. So when Lucas paused, asking if we had any questions, I raised my hand, my throat tightening at the thought of speaking it aloud. But I had to. Had to know.

"Maybe I missed it, but for all the time the philosophers spent talking about making the right choice, none of them ever talked about *how* to do it when the choices are hard."

"What kinds of choices are you thinking about, Ms. Renfield?"

I pretended to think, then took a deep breath and asked it. "Let's say you somehow knew someone was about to die." My stomach was in knots as I finally said aloud what I'd barely been willing to ask myself. "Should you tell them? Or not? What's the right thing to do?" Everyone was looking at me.

Lucas frowned. "You know they're about to die? What do you mean? Like a doctor who can see a cancer?"

Not what I had in mind, but that would do. "Sure."

He nodded. "Well, I think both Aristotle and Kant would say the doctor's responsibility is clear: to tell the patient so they could explore treatment options."

"What if there were no treatment options? The cancer was too far along, definitely fatal."

"I think they'd say it's still the doctor's responsibility to tell the patient."

"Why?"

"So the person can decide how to spend their remaining time."

"Why is that the better course? If there's no cure and happiness is the greatest good, wouldn't it be better for the doctor to let the patient live in happiness?"

Lucas thought for a moment. "Well. Incurable diseases are not painless. The person would be suffering and has come to the doctor for an answer. The doctor's role is to provide health. In this case, maybe he can't provide physical health, but he could provide mental rest by telling the patient the truth. It is what the patient has come seeking. It is the doctor's duty to provide it."

"Okay." I paused, regrouping. This wasn't going the way I wanted it to. "What if the patient hadn't come seeking it?"

"How could that be?"

"Well . . . let's say the patient doesn't feel any pain. They're just at the doctor for a routine physical, but the doctor finds this incurable cancer, widespread. Untreatable. The patient is totally unaware of a problem. If there's nothing that can be done for the patient—their physical health can't be improved and their mental health may be harmed by the news—what is the doctor's responsibility?"

Lucas looked at me hard, a small smile at the corners of his mouth. "What an interesting dilemma, Ms. Renfield. Let's ask the class."

Cop-out, I thought. I waited for Professor McMillan to jump in and answer, but he only watched as hands shot up around the room. For a while, I listened to the discussion, but my classmates gave me nothing. I'd already covered every scenario, every opinion they had, on my own.

Plato had talked about reconciling what we knew we *should* do with our fear of doing it and our desire to do something else. But his arguments assumed I knew what I should do. I didn't. Same with Kant—I couldn't do my duty if I didn't know what it was.

It was frustrating. Throughout the room, students were debating, some passionately—definitely our best discussion so far. Great. The abstract was fun in class, but I wanted the concrete in my life. I needed, as Aristotle said, a target to aim at. It made me think of Tasha standing in her garage, facing the concentric circles of the hay-bound target what felt like a hundred years ago. I wished I could go back there, challenge her to a winner-takes-all round of archery, the stakes nothing more than coffee and a chocolate chip muffin from Jake's Deli.

Around me, zippers were being opened, papers rustling, books snapping shut. At the front of the room, Professor McMillan reminded us of our assignment for the next week. "Great discussion," he said as people started to file out of the room. "Ms. Renfield, thank you for getting us started."

I gave him a quick nod and hurried past. Outside the classroom, I caught the end of one girl's comment to her friend: "... Lucas Canton? Totally choiceworthy."

chapter 16

He walked into Cuppa the next day, as I was finishing my shift.
Instead of going to Doug at the counter, Lucas came to my station, resting his tanned arms on the high granite surface of
the bar.

"You have to place your order over there," I told him, trying
to ignore the way my heartbeat had suddenly gone staccato. "No
special deals, not even for my TA."

"I came to see you. Can I take you to dinner?"

My stuttering heart felt like it had stopped. I looked quickly
at Doug, stalling for composure, but he was busy counting the till.
"Tonight?"

"You're almost finished here, right?" And, in fact, I was. He
had timed it as if he knew my schedule.

Lucas waited for me on a bench outside, which was a relief. I
didn't want to talk about him with Doug, or worse, not talk about

him and just let the awkwardness of my maybe-date hang in the air. I could picture Doug's raised eyebrows and disappointed eyes, the lower lid wincing ever so slightly. But he never noticed Lucas, which meant I never had to explain why I was leaving with him when I'd never been willing to even have lunch with Doug, who'd really been nothing but wonderful since I'd met him.

"What are you reading?"

I'd startled Lucas, totally immersed in the tattered pages of his paperback. Watching him unguarded in the seconds between the door and the bench, I thought I could see how he'd been in high school: quiet, shy, too serious, but gorgeous behind the glasses and thick books. He seemed the kind of boy girls had secret crushes on because he was just a little too distant to encourage them. I wondered if he'd gone to homecoming or prom and who his best friend had been.

He smiled and flipped the cover closed to hold it up: *A Prayer for Owen Meany.*

I was glad to see a novel instead of something academic. "Great book."

He nodded. "I think this is my third time through it." Lucas marked his page with a dog-eared corner, then slid it into the worn messenger bag he carried to class. "You like Italian?" He stood, less than a foot from me, and I could smell his aftershave, clean and crisp like a breezy day at the beach. Intoxicating.

"Sure," I answered, perfectly hiding how my pulse raced at his closeness.

"A friend of mine owns a place just a few blocks away," he said as we started walking. "Mostly Northern Italian. Delicious."

It was that part of summer where days go on forever. Nearly eight o'clock and the streetlights were hardly needed. I'd been nervous that it would be awkward with Lucas, but our conversation danced lightly over common ground. Something about the evening, the long, easy days of summer, made me feel like it would have been perfectly natural for him to slip his hand in mine as we strolled the comfortable sidewalks of Bering. He didn't. But I kept hoping he might.

The restaurant was on a side street that I'd never been down.

"Gianna," he said, returning the owner's air-kiss greeting, "this is Cassandra."

"So nice to meet you." Gianna had a trace of an accent and a warm smile. She led us to a courtyard table in back. "Please. Let me know if you need anything. Wallace will be with you in a moment."

There were four other tables, only two of them occupied, surrounding a small stone fountain on the patio. Candlelit sconces and flickering lights on each table made it feel secret and intimate. If it hadn't been owned by his friend, choosing someplace like this would have left me no doubt about Lucas's intentions.

Our waiter appeared with bread and water and Lucas ordered a carafe of wine.

"You're not twenty-one," I said when the waiter left.

"No, but Gianna would be disappointed if we didn't have a glass with dinner." He smiled. "It's the Italian way."

I thought about our lesson from last week, Socrates preferring death to breaking the laws of Athens, then shook my head. Too much philosophy on the brain.

"So, how do you know Gianna?" I asked.

"She's a friend of my mother's, actually. Years ago, she owned a bakery back home. Gianna and her husband moved here when he got a job running Food Services at the U. When I decided to come to Lennox, my mom and she reconnected." He reached across the table for the butter, his hand nearly brushing mine. "Gianna's a great cook, but a fantastic baker. You have to try the desserts. They're amazing."

The wine came and Lucas and I watched Wallace fill both our glasses midway. We ordered our meals and Lucas raised his glass, his eyes meeting mine. "Cheers."

"Cheers," I agreed, clinking his rim softly.

He'd chosen a merlot, fruity and warm. I sipped gently, familiar enough with alcohol from Nan's tea and the occasional holiday toast to know how quickly it can go to your head.

"So, are you enjoying our class?"

"I am," I answered. "It's challenging, as you said it would be, but I like it." I sipped again, looking up at him as I added, "I thought you were good yesterday."

He smiled. "I thought you were good yesterday too. I can't say that was in my lesson plan, but that's the fun thing about philosophy. You never know when you're going to get a great back-and-forth going."

I took a piece of the bread he offered. "How'd you wind up majoring in it? It's kind of an unusual choice."

"Yeah." Lucas shrugged, flashing a small, embarrassed smile. "My mom went through a Buddhist phase when I was in high school. You know, Zen, karma, the whole thing. It got me thinking about why we're here. I took a few classes back home and was hooked." He paused, looking down as he added, softer, "I think we all have a purpose in life. I guess I'm just trying to figure out exactly what mine is."

I'd never heard a guy be so honest. Maybe Jack, but only about small things. There was a vulnerability about the way Lucas said it that made me feel warm and trusted and special, like we were cocooned here in this quiet place together. I took another sip of the wine, letting his words sink in. Purpose. I didn't really want to think about the mark, but for once, it seemed like the right time to bring it up and Lucas the right person.

I watched him carefully as I said, "You know, you never answered the question in class yesterday."

"About . . . ?"

"The doctor's responsibility. You tossed it out to the group but never gave your opinion."

He answered without hesitation. "I think the doctor should tell what he knows."

"Why?"

"Remember what Aristotle said about using pain correctly? The path to happiness isn't always fun." He leaned in, his closeness making my head a little fuzzy. "But dealing with hard things, like a terminal diagnosis, can lead to greater happiness. No pain, no gain."

I thought of the woman in the park playing with her dog.

"But what if time was so short . . ." I stopped, knowing it would be nearly impossible to convey the full scenario. Lucas would think it was ridiculous.

"Go on . . . so short that . . ."

I shook my head. "Nothing. It's just a hypothetical."

"Isn't all of this?"

"Yeah . . . but this couldn't really happen."

He leaned back, smiling. "Try me anyway. I'm interested."

I could tell, his eyes, his attention totally focused on me. It was a thrilling feeling that I didn't want to let go. "Okay," I said, "what if time was so short that there was really nothing the person could do? What if they had less than twenty-four hours to live, were in no pain, totally unaware of their fate and enjoying their time." I decided to go for it. "What if they were spending a beautiful day outside, in the sun, playing with their dog or their child? Would you interrupt that day with the news that they were about to die?"

"I thought they were at the doctor's office."

I rolled my eyes. "Maybe they were in the park that morning, before their appointment."

"And the doctor figures out they're going to die that day? That couldn't happen."

"That's why I said it was a hypothetical." I shook my head. "Forget it."

"No, no. Okay, I'm with you." He thought for a minute. "I'm not sure."

"Maybe it's a case-by-case thing?" I suggested hopefully. "If the person seems fine, untroubled, you don't tell them?"

"No, I don't think so," Lucas said, pinching his lip absently. "How could the doctor really know their state of mind? Or how they might use the news that they had such a short time to live? Maybe there were things that had to be done to secure happiness for the child or someone else important."

I nodded. I had thought that too, and had a creeping suspicion that the right answer was the one I didn't really want. The harder choice.

Our dinners came then. Lucas was right, the food was delicious. I hadn't been doing much cooking at the apartment. I'd learned the basics from Nan and together we'd made lasagnas and stews and soups and fish. I'd come to associate cooking with companionship.

It wasn't the same doing it alone and just for me, so I'd been living on easy meals like a true college student: tuna fish, cheese sandwiches, pizza—sometimes takeout, sometimes frozen.

"Now, this . . . ," I said in between mouthfuls, shaking my fork at the half-empty plate. "This is food."

"An astute observation," Lucas said, his grin making me smile too. "See, I knew you were smart . . ."

Lucas asked about my job, told me a little about his. The behind-the-scenes work of a teaching assistant sounded like a lot of reading, lesson plans, and pipe smoking with Professor McMillan.

When we'd finished our meal, Wallace took our plates and our tiramisu order—one to share. Lucas poured the last of the wine, leaned back, and asked, "What would you do with your final hours if you knew you only had a few to live?"

"I think," I said slowly, giving the impression of contemplating, "my first impulse would be to find another doctor—and another after that, if necessary—and try to prevent it."

He nodded. "For the sake of discussion, let's assume the diagnosis was irrefutable and somehow you accepted that."

"Okay," I said. "I think my next impulse would be to do something crazy—try to squeeze in some of the things I'd meant to do but never got around to. See the Eiffel Tower or Statue of Liberty. Go bungee jumping. The problem with having only a few hours, though, is that it's too short to accomplish anything important. No time for the life goals you haven't made happen yet, whatever they are: write a book, have a family, try out for Broadway."

"Those are your life goals?"

"Not mine personally, but you know what I mean. The kind of things that take work and planning."

He nodded. "So you'd take a trip somewhere on your last day?"

"No," I corrected. "That would be my first impulse, but I think I'd realize all the problems with it. I mean, what if my flight were delayed? Would I want to spend my final hours sitting in an airport? Just to see some building somewhere?"

Lucas waited, quietly fingering the stem of his wineglass and watching me intently.

What I'd thought about most the many times I'd considered this question was how Nan had reacted: calm, fully in control. I hoped I could be that way.

"I think what I'd really do—and this may sound nuts—is nothing. I mean, there'd be a little business to take care of. I'd write a few letters, make sure I got them in a mailbox, and then I'd take my book and my favorite sweatshirt and find a comfortable spot—the park or a coffee shop—and try to enjoy the time I had left."

Lucas was silent for a minute, still watching me, still fingering his glass. "That's a very rational response," he said finally.

I shrugged. "Well, it's one thing to say it and another to act it out. Who knows how I'd really be."

He didn't say anything, so I asked, "What would you do?"

Without hesitation, he said, "I'd take the first flight to LA."

"To see your family?"

"To see my family."

I nodded. I might have said the same thing if I had any family to see.

We finished our wine with dessert. The tiramisu was amazing, as Lucas had promised. When the bill came, Lucas deftly took it from the waiter, shooing away my offers to go Dutch. "Of course not," he said. "I asked you to dinner. Besides, you're a poor college student."

"So are you."

"Oh. Right." He handed Wallace an American Express card. Gold. While we waited, I took another look at our courtyard. The other tables had cleared and we were alone with the gentle gurgle of the fountain, candles all around. I could feel Lucas looking at me and turned to him.

"What?" I demanded.

"Nothing," he answered, smiling. "You're an interesting girl, Cassandra Renfield. How old are you?"

Maybe I should have told Lucas the truth. But I was afraid it would shatter the perfection of this moment, the best I'd had in way too long. So I didn't. "Eighteen."

He shook his head. "You're the oldest eighteen I've ever met."

I didn't know what to say to that.

Gianna kissed us each on the cheek as we left, telling Lucas not to be a stranger. To me, she said she hoped I'd be back. She sounded like she meant it.

We walked to the main street, the lamps lighting the now-empty sidewalks in oblong circles. We were close, but not touching. I didn't know what to expect from Lucas. I'd never been out like this—a real dinner date, if that's what this was. I wasn't a complete innocent, but high school dates were fast food and football and movies and the mall, not this. I wasn't even sure I was really on a date. What if Lucas just thought I was interesting? A student to mentor?

And then he said, "My place is just down the block. You want to come up for a nightcap?"

He'd put on an accent like in the old movies Nan used to watch, winking and raising one eyebrow. It was silly and completely charming. I felt like I might scream or faint. In a good way. "I don't wear one," I managed to answer.

"Ba-dum-bump."

We stood there: Lucas smiling down at me, nonchalant, my stomach doing flip-flops. What would happen if I went? What if I didn't? Would I ever get another chance?

"Is that okay?" I asked, my voice calmer than I felt. Thank God for the wine. "I mean with me in class, you the TA . . ."

"I think I clear the ethics board," he said. "After all, you're not taking the class for credit, right?"

"True."

"Therefore, you are not being graded and I hold no sway over you. You stand to gain nothing by befriending me."

"If I would be the one gaining, why would you be held accountable by an ethics board?"

He smiled again. "Excellent question."

He took my hand and led me to an old brick building down another quiet side street. I felt everything—Lucas's firm, hot grip, the slight breeze, a spinning dizziness that was the wine and him all wrapped together. I took a deep breath, inhaling the warm night air to steady myself as we ascended his steps and went inside.

chapter 17

He was sitting on the edge of the bed, watching me when I woke up.

"What time is it?" I asked, automatically looking at my naked wrist, my watch somewhere on his nightstand.

"Shh," he said. "Early. Just before eight." He stroked my hair and it felt wonderful. I closed my eyes. "I didn't want to wake you," he said softly, "but I have an early meeting at school."

I started to get up. "I have to work anyway."

He shook his head. "No rush, Cassandra. Take your time, as long as you like. Just push the lock on the door when you go."

I propped myself on an elbow and looked at him, my eyes better adjusted to the light. He was amazing, I thought, his hair brushing the rims of his glasses. He smiled.

"I had a nice time last night," he said. "Can I see you again?"

I smiled too, self-conscious about being this way—lying rumpled in his bed. "I'd like that," I said, trying to sound like a college girl might.

He leaned over and kissed my forehead. I watched him leave,

my TA, his familiar bag slung over one shoulder. A shoulder that I had seen, had touched bare.

I flopped back in bed, reveling in the warm, tingly feeling inside. I was really here, I thought, in Lucas's apartment. I had kissed Lucas and . . . well, other stuff. I was a little embarrassed to think about that.

I sat up, looking around his space, dying to learn more, know everything about him. I pulled on my sweater and walked to the living room, liking the scratchy feel of its straw rug on my bare feet. There was a stack of hardback books on his coffee table. I leaned sideways to read their spines: *Our Century in Pictures, Ancient Greece, World Atlas.* There were more books on shelves along the wall. Books everywhere, I realized. A short stack of paperbacks on the end table, another near the window, another on his desk beside three picture frames.

I walked over to look at the photos. One was obviously Lucas's family. Beautiful people on a beach near sunset. His mom and dad were gray-haired, but trim and smiling. Holding hands, of all things.

The second was Lucas with a group of girls and guys. I recognized one, the pretty blonde from the coffee shop. The picture looked recent, had been taken on campus. She was next to him, his arm around her shoulder. I looked closely, but the meaning was unclear. The whole feel of the picture was casual, friendly. Still, I wondered, having seen them together at Cuppa more than once. I was jealous, but felt stupid for feeling so. After all, I was here and she wasn't, right?

The last photo was a little older. Lucas in high school, I guessed. Surrounded by other guys, all of them in faded sweatshirts, a football slung in one's arm. It took me a minute to find

Lucas without his glasses and made me wonder about my initial impressions of him. Here he didn't look the quiet bookworm any more than the jock I sat next to in philosophy.

I checked the clock and realized I needed to get going to be at Cuppa by ten. I still had to get back to the apartment for a shower and change of clothes. Drea would be at work, not that it mattered. I'd been worried last night, but her response to my text telling her I was staying with a friend from class had been a cavalier "Have fun." Some guardian.

On my way out, I took one more look at Lucas's home, his personal space. I hoped I'd be back, but just in case, I wanted one final memory. Then I pushed in the button on the slim side of the door, checking the knob to be sure it would lock, and closed it carefully behind me.

chapter 18

I shouldn't have worried that my first visit to Lucas's might be my only one. In fact, I spent so much time there in the weeks following our dinner at Gianna's that it felt more like home than Drea's.

Since Nan had died, I thought I'd come to like being on my own, which is basically what I was. Aside from her one tipsy night, Drea's conversations with me had barely moved beyond "We're out of Cheerios" and "Don't forget to turn the fans off when you leave." Spending time with Lucas now made me realize I'd been kidding myself. I'd been lonely. Really lonely. It was so nice to have someone to eat dinner with or walk beside in the park or just lie near, reading on the sofa. My hours, instead of inching along, seemed almost too short. And the mark, though it never left my mind completely, was less consuming. A soft tap on the shoulder rather than a constant, throbbing squeeze.

I guess I kind of knew all along. That's why I'd thought—briefly—about going out with Doug when he'd asked. I'd needed someone, but not just anyone. Lucas.

I wrote to Tasha about him. We e-mailed more than we spoke now, and it felt funny, almost like writing in a diary—intimate, but disconnected.

I'm dating my philosophy TA. He's smart, gorgeous, so nice.
It's only been a couple weeks, but it's going great. This
might be the L-thing.

I couldn't even bring myself to write the word. Afraid to admit that I really felt that way about someone older and more sophisticated. It was hard to believe that a few weeks ago, Lucas had been a customer in the coffee shop, my TA that maybe I had a little crush on. He'd become so much more in the short time we'd been together, our relationship compressed like Philosophy 101— so much squished into so little time. It made any feelings I might have had for Jack Petroski seem silly and juvenile. This was a real relationship. With a top hat, Nan would have said. All grown-up.

We went out to dinners—at Gianna's and other places. Often Lucas waited for me at Cuppa near the end of my shift.

"Your boyfriend is outside," Doug said one day. My face turned pink at the word, especially on Doug's lips.

"Thanks."

"He teaches at the school, right?" Doug was standing beside me now, his voice a touch strident. Or maybe I imagined it.

"Sort of. He's just a sophomore, but doing a teaching assistant thing for the summer."

"Yeah. I've seen him in here before." Doug nodded, casually polishing the cappuccino machine nearby. I willed a customer to come in, but the door stayed shut, the faint jingling of the bells only the wind. "Before you started here, actually, he used to come in a lot with a girl. Pretty. Blond."

"Oh yeah?" I tried to match Doug's nonchalant tone. I think it was a strain for both of us.

He shrugged. "They were probably just friends. Have you met her?"

"No."

"Well, maybe it was something else," he said. Then, more kindly, "That was a while ago."

The fact is, I hadn't really met any of Lucas's friends. I had asked him about his pictures, not about her in particular, but the group. The other students in the summer TA program, he'd told me, which meant I might never meet her. Lucas and I didn't hide our relationship, but we didn't advertise it either. On campus and, of course, in class we kept our distance. I would gladly have left philosophy hand in hand with him—wouldn't have minded showing the girls in my class who Lucas thought was choiceworthy—but I understood, without discussion, that Professor McMillan might not think it okay for me to be his girlfriend, audit student or not.

In the comfortable hours at his apartment, I fantasized about moving in with him. I doodled *Cassandra Canton* in my notebooks, liking the alliterative sound of it whispered aloud, then quickly scribbled it out before Lucas could see that I wasn't the deep thinker he took me for, but just a silly schoolgirl after all.

Sometimes, reading my texts, highlighting and underlining, I'd look up to find him watching me. It made my heart race.

He liked discussing our lessons before class, arguing out the philosophies. It was a habit from our first dinner together that stuck. We agreed on Locke, but I frustrated him with Descartes.

"How can you take him seriously," I argued, "when he says things like 'Because God has given me my understanding, all I understand, I understand correctly'? There are a gazillion holes in that."

"Cassandra, you have to consider the context . . ."

"No. I can't get past his 'God this, God that.' Plus, he's a coward. His whole idea that you shouldn't use your free will if you don't understand something fully? Come on, Lucas, there would be no progress if everyone believed that."

"He didn't mean we shouldn't take chances," Lucas corrected, "just that we should expect mistakes because our understanding is weaker than our will."

Lucas was incredibly well-read, always bringing bits of science or history or religion into our discussions. In class we had just started the section on determinism—the idea that there is no chance or choice—and Lucas and I were hashing out William James's Divinity Street, Oxford Avenue problem. Once William James chose to walk down Divinity Street, there was no way to prove whether it was fate or free will that made him do it. He couldn't test whether he'd had equal freedom to choose Oxford Avenue because he could never put himself in the exact same situation again. I was trying to wrap my head around the idea and what it could mean for the mark. I would have liked to ask Lucas, but I didn't want him to think I was weird, bringing up my doctor-and-patient scenario again.

"You know," Lucas said, leaning back in the nook of the sofa opposite me. "The ancient Greeks were the original determinists. They believed your fate was decided from the time you were born."

"So William James knew which street he'd walk down even before he could walk?"

Lucas nodded. "Something like that. The Greeks personified fate in three gods, goddesses actually, that controlled people's destinies, spun the thread of their fate at birth."

"So they planned which street he'd walk down?" I persisted.

Lucas shrugged. "Ultimately, yes."

"And what I'd eat for breakfast today? Or which shoes I'd wear? You know, I wish they'd clue me in, 'cause some mornings I really struggle . . ."

Lucas frowned. "Bigger picture, Cassandra. Life and death."

"I'm just kidding, Lucas. Nan liked those myths, used to tell me the stories," I said. "She gave me a book about them for my sixteenth birthday, just a little . . ." I'd been about to say "before she died," catching myself just in time. I still hadn't told Lucas my real age, couldn't imagine doing it now. "Just a little book," I finished. "Very old. A family heirloom. It had belonged to my mother. Of course, it was in Greek, so it was kind of hard to read."

"Oh yeah?"

"Yeah. It's back in Ashville somewhere. She got me other ones too. In English. She was into that stuff. Part of the heritage or whatever. Not my kind of stories."

"You know, they weren't just stories, Cass. This was a religion. It's like calling the Bible a story."

I shrugged. "That's not really my kind of story either."

The only time we didn't hash out the readings was before classes Lucas was to teach. He didn't want a preview of the things that might be thrown at him, preferring the harder road of having to think on his feet. I admired that, but never challenged him in class anyway. I don't think I could have had a public argument without turning absolutely magenta, sure that everyone would see the way I felt about him.

We were halfway through summer session, a week past the July 4 break. Halfway through my time with Drea too, though I no longer counted the days. Not with an eye toward their conclusion, at least. Lucas and I had been together just over a month, though it felt like much longer. He was already pushing me to take a class or two for credit in fall and apply as a full-time student for next year. I had gotten the paperwork and was thinking about looking into it, maybe trying for my GED or something, asking Drea if I could stay. Crazy ideas, really. Mostly I tried not to think about the future. We have time, I thought, I'll just enjoy today and figure out the rest later.

chapter 19

I could feel his weight beside me, warm and comforting, before I opened my eyes. The honking outside meant it was rush hour in Bering, past eight, time to get up. I rolled over to face Lucas. It was one of my favorite things, to catch him in that moment just before waking when his face was between the slackness of sleep and its daytime consciousness.

But there was something wrong with that face. I rubbed my eyes, praying it was a trick of the light, always overbright in his south-facing, whitewashed rooms.

The mark on Lucas didn't go away.

I sat up, grabbing my head in both hands. There was no reason for it to be his time. Couldn't be.

"Cass?" Lucas rolled onto his back, rubbing his eyes sleepily. "Timesit?"

I couldn't answer. What would I say? *Eight twelve* seemed too mundane. *Less than twenty-four hours before you die* too dramatic.

"C'sandra?" Lucas propped himself on his elbows, squinting at me. "You okay?"

I nodded. What to do? What to do? A million thoughts raced through my head—get him to a hospital—or should it be on a plane to California? No, a hospital was no good. For God's sake, he was eighteen; he wasn't going to have a heart attack. It was going to be an accident. I thought about all the things that could happen: plane crashes, car wrecks, Wile E. Coyote anvil to the head. I realized that there was no sun streaming through his blinds and hopped off the bed to pull them aside. Raining. I remembered Mr. McKenzie, the squealing tires, the awful crunch. Right.

"Let's stay in today," I said.

He smiled, sat up, and rubbed his eyes again. "I'd love to, Cassandra. But I've got to get to this TA work session."

"Skip it."

He shook his head. "No can do. It's mandatory and there're only ten of us. I would definitely be missed."

"Tell them you're sick. I'll call in to the coffee shop and we'll stay here together."

He looked at me closer. "You sure you're okay?"

"I'm fine." *But you're not.* I had to convince him to stay. It was the only chance. What could possibly happen here? Immediately, a list of things popped into my mind: gas explosion, roof collapse, building fire. Still, it was safer than the outside world. But how to keep him in? If I told him the truth, he'd think I was crazy. Or he might run out the door, to the airport. Wasn't that his right, though? To choose how to spend his last day?

I tried again. "Come on. Let's do something spontaneous. Carpe diem. We'll order breakfast, maybe read . . . I don't know, sonnets aloud to each other or . . ."

He held up a hand. "I'd love to, honey, but today's not a good day. Let's carpe diem tomorrow, when I don't have a meeting."

Lucas pushed aside the down comforter and stood, stretching his smooth and muscular body. "I'm going to hop in the shower." And off he went.

I sat on the edge of the bed, trying to figure out what to do. I couldn't let Lucas go. The thought of losing him was a buzzing pressure swelling my brain, making it hard to hear or see. It couldn't be his day. I wouldn't let it. But I knew his tone: he was committed to that stupid meeting. I thought of telling him I was sick or calling in a bomb threat, but in the end, I couldn't be sure any of them would really keep him here.

When he came out of the shower, still steamy, with a towel wrapped around his waist and another rubbing his hair, I was waiting.

He stopped short when he saw me.

"Lucas, I have to tell you something. Something you're going to think is crazy."

He stared at me, worry creasing the space between his brows.

I took a deep breath. "There's this thing, kind of a sixth sense that I have." I had never said it aloud to anyone but Nan, and hearing the words in my head, just before they came out, they sounded nuts. "I can tell when someone is about to die."

No reaction.

I rushed on, needing to get it out before it was too late, before he cut me off or I started to cry. "It's something I see—a light, like a glow—around them. It's been there as far back as I can remember. When I see it, they die that day. I can't tell how it's going to happen, or exactly when, just that, as far as I know, it's before the day ends."

Still nothing.

I whispered the next part. "I see it on you. Right now."

He didn't speak, didn't move, and neither did I. Outside, life went on, horns honked, doors slammed, but here nothing, both of us paralyzed. Me by the magnitude of what I'd told him, and Lucas by . . . I'm not sure what. The complete unbelievability of it maybe.

"You're kidding, right?" He knew I wasn't.

I shook my head.

"You really believe this? That you can see . . . death?"

I nodded and said softly, "I can." And then I started crying. It was so God-awful important to me that Lucas believe and not leave me, and I could tell I wasn't getting through to him. That, at best, he thought I was hysterical and at worse, psycho, someone he should have known better than to get involved with in the first place. I couldn't win.

He came to me, put his hands on my shoulders. "Cassie."

I couldn't look at him. I looked down, but even his feet were surrounded by the damned light. I closed my eyes, the tears squeezing through somehow, running unchecked down my cheeks. He wiped them.

"I don't know what to think of this, but if it's that important to you, I'll stay."

My entire body flooded with relief. I looked up, hoping the light would be gone, that—decision made—it would evaporate. It didn't.

"You don't . . ." I didn't want to say it, but felt like I had to. "You don't want to go to LA, do you?"

Lucas looked confused for a minute, then almost smiled, but his grin quickly disappeared. "No, Cass. I want to stay here, with you."

I nodded. That was good enough for now.

We dressed and sat on the sofa, trying to read, the space between us huge. I kept looking at him, nervous every time he moved to go to the bathroom or get a drink or turn down the music. Every action seemed fraught with danger.

Ten o'clock passed, then eleven, twelve. I made lunch. Soup. Nothing with lumps or bones. Afterward, Lucas stretched and bent, eyeing the door.

"How long do we have to keep this up, Cassandra? How 'bout I run to the store for some provisions?"

I shook my head and reluctantly he returned to the sofa.

Around three thirty, Lucas went to the bathroom. I counted the minutes he was in there, another wave of relief when I heard the knob turn.

I stared at him, blinking twice, sure I was wrong. "What did you do in there?" I demanded.

He looked startled. "I answered the call of nature, Cassandra. You want details?"

"Maybe."

"Listen," he said, rubbing his brow. "I'm trying to be a good sport, but I've about had it. This is . . ."

"Lucas," I said, afraid to even speak the words, afraid to believe. "It's gone."

"Huh?"

"The light, the mark. It's gone. It was there when you went into the bathroom. Now it's not. What did you do in there?"

"Nothing, Cassandra. I went in. I peed. I came out. That's it."

"Nothing else?" I demanded, though I couldn't imagine what else there might be. Had he rescued himself from a burst bladder? Taken a life-saving dose of pills? Ridiculous.

"Nothing else," he assured me.

We stayed in the rest of the day, cautiously treading around each other. I held my breath, watching Lucas constantly for any sign of its reappearance. It felt like the weight had been lifted but hovered just above my shoulders, ready to slam back down if I exhaled. We went to bed early that night, me, exhausted by the vigil, and Lucas, sadly, tired of me. I felt the absence of his arm around me, his weight firmly situated on the other side of the mattress. But I had saved him, I thought, in awe of my own ability. The rest could be repaired.

chapter 20

The mark stayed gone, though the few minutes of sleep I got that night were run through with nightmarish visions of it, screeching car brakes, and Lucas's wary looks. On top of that, I had Drea to worry about.

"Don't you think you've been out a lot?" she'd said on my voice mail. "Where's your friend's apartment? I can pick you up." I didn't call back. Of all times to play parent, she chooses now? I don't think so.

As the dark slowly crept to day—black to navy to cornflower blue—I lay on Lucas's bed, careful not to wake him. Near seven his eyes fluttered, opening to find me staring at him. He didn't say anything.

"Good morning," I whispered.

"Good morning."

"It's still gone," I assured him.

He just stared at me, and I knew the wary looks were here to stay.

"You don't believe me."

Lucas rolled to his back and ran a hand through his hair, exhaling. "Cassie." His voice was that of an adult reasoning with a child. "C'mon. How could I?"

"It's the truth, Lucas."

He nodded, still not looking at me. "I believe that you believe it."

"You think I'm crazy." He shut his eyes. "Do I seem like the crazy type?"

No answer.

"Say something, Lucas." There was a little panic in my voice. I couldn't keep it out, though it was the last way I wanted to have this conversation. He needed to believe, because the alternative . . . well, I couldn't handle the alternative.

"What do you want me to say, Cassie?"

"I'll prove it to you."

He propped himself on one arm, facing me skeptically. "How?"

"The same way I proved it to myself. We'll find someone with the mark and follow them."

"Cassie, that's . . . We don't have to do that."

"Yes. We do. Listen, Lucas, I know how it sounds, but I'm not crazy. Even if you don't believe, humor me. One more time."

"Let me get this straight." He sat up, keeping a careful distance. "You want to wander the streets until you see someone with this . . . this light around them and then we'll follow them until they die."

I pictured Mr. McKenzie and my stomach did a slow roll. I'd never wanted to see something like that again, couldn't imagine why I'd have to. I clenched my teeth and nodded. "That's right."

He thought about it and shrugged. "Okay, Cassandra. Let's go."

I shook my head. "Not in Bering. It could be weeks before I see another here. We need to go somewhere bigger, with more people."

"So you want to skip class and go to the city—to Wichita—today?"

I thought about how it had looked when I'd flown in: a bunch of office buildings, even a skyscraper or two around a big domed building, like a flying saucer. I nodded. "That should do it."

Lucas had called Professor McMillan, claiming a persistent stomach bug. "I'm sure I'll be back on my feet tomorrow," he'd told him, frowning at me as he spoke. We were mostly silent on the two-hour drive. The empty cornfields rushing by should have been hypnotic, but my brain was on overdrive. I was convinced Lucas had been meant to have an accident, something outside the safety of the apartment. But, if so, why hadn't the mark left when he said he'd stay? Had he not really meant it? Or had some other more definite milestone passed, like the actual moment of his fated death? Was there something else Lucas decided to do or not do, maybe not even realizing it? It made me wonder about the hundreds of decisions that make up a day. How did my choice of muffin or hairstyle change my day and all the days after? What would be the result of our taking this trip to Wichita rather than going to work and school as we were supposed to?

My mind was busy with unanswerable questions, keeping me from acknowledging the most awesome and awful one—had I really changed fate?

* * *

We got there around twelve. Lunchtime. Perfect.

"Drive toward the buildings," I told him.

Lucas found parking on the street, squeezing his car into a just-big-enough spot. "We've got to feed the meter," he said. "How long do you want to stay?"

I had already started scanning the people on the street, feeling jittery and distracted. "Whatever you think."

"I have no idea, Cassandra," he said shortly. "You tell me. How long will we be here?"

"I don't know, Lucas. How about two hours? Three?" I figured if I was going to see one, it would happen now, while all the businesspeople were out, getting their lunch and running errands.

He dropped the coins in and waited for me to lead the way. We walked down the wide sidewalks, trying to stay in the shade, little protection from the blazing July heat that seemed worse here, contained by concrete. People walked slower in the Midwest than they had in Pennsylvania, groups of suited men and women meandering to cafés, delis, and restaurants.

Lucas and I followed, crisscrossing streets aimlessly until I found a small park that seemed near the center of things.

"Let's just sit for a little," I told him. "This'll be a good spot to watch."

We sat. And sat. And sat.

"Mind if I read?" Lucas asked after we'd been there nearly an hour.

I shrugged. What did it matter? He didn't need to see anything. I had tried a little conversation, but Lucas was not a willing participant and I was too anxious to work at it. People were everywhere, even more than I'd have expected on such a hot day. Men and women shed suit jackets to linger by the benches, talking on cell phones or in groups of twos and threes. There were older people too, with crossword puzzles and crumbs for the city birds. Mothers strolled by, kids played ball. I must have seen hundreds of people in the two and a half hours we were there, all of them perfectly dull. Not a sign of the mark.

Lucas laid aside his papers with a sigh. "Nothing, huh?" His tone told me it was exactly as he'd suspected.

"No. Sometimes it's like this, Lucas. It can be weeks, months, between times that I see it . . ."

"Uh-huh."

"Maybe we should go to a hospital. I mean, there's sure to be someone there . . ."

"And do what, Cassandra? Wander the halls, poking into all the rooms? What are you going to say you're doing there, assuming you can even get past security and onto a floor?"

He was right, of course. I remembered the layers of checkpoints from my visits to Nan.

He sighed again and glanced at his watch. "Listen, why don't we hit the road? It's a long—"

"Cassie?" another voice interrupted. I looked up, startled. It took me a minute to adjust to the glare of the sun over his right shoulder. I hadn't seen him approaching, only looking for light, not faces. How he picked me out, I can't imagine. The unlikeliest of people in the unlikeliest place.

"Oh my God," I gasped. "Jack Petroski."

I stood and he bent to give me a hug, our heads bumping awkwardly.

"Ouch!" I rubbed my forehead.

He smiled. "What on earth are you doing here?" He looked great, his tanned face scruffy where I was used to seeing him clean-shaven. It made him seem a little rougher, older.

"I . . . uh . . . I'm staying here. Well, not here, but in Kansas. Bering. It's a town two hours or so north of here. And we . . ." I had forgotten about Lucas, who was watching us, a little amused, mostly annoyed. "This is Lucas," I said belatedly. "My boyfriend."

"Nice to meet you." Jack offered his hand.

Lucas shook it, but didn't stand.

"What are *you* doing here?" I asked quickly. Lucas looked back down at his papers, but I could tell he wasn't reading.

"Visiting Wichita State. My parents are back on campus with the financial people and I'm meeting up with some of the guys from the baseball program who're still around. Kind of a tour of the town thing."

"They have a good team?"

"One of the best. And they really seem to want me."

"That's awesome, Jack. I'm so happy for you." We stood there, smiling at each other stupidly. If Lucas hadn't been listening to every word, there were a million things I'd have asked Jack. It was so good to see someone from home. To see him.

"So." Jack looked a little more serious, oblivious to the awkwardness of Lucas being so close. "Is this where you came when you disappeared?"

I nodded, surprised he would put it like that. Surprised he'd noticed, really. I mean, school had been almost over. I was sure Jack would have been wrapped up in exams, State finals, that kind of stuff.

"I wondered about you. I was kind of worried, to tell you the truth."

I smiled, but felt a pinprick of tears. "Why?"

He shrugged. "I just remember the last time we talked. After Nan. I could tell how hard it was for you . . ."

I remembered too. The warmth of Jack's sweatshirt. The clean, earthy smell. "Yeah, well, it's better now."

He smiled. "I guess. You look great."

Lucas stood then. "We should get going, Cassandra. It's a long drive back."

"Right." I glanced at him, could tell he was pissed. I didn't know whether it was about Jack or the day or what. I turned back to Jack, wanting to stay, wondering about seeing him here, about fate dealing me this rather than what I'd come looking for. "It was great to see you," I told him.

"You too, Cassie. When're you coming back? I mean . . ." He glanced at Lucas. "You are coming back, right?"

"Sure," I said, not at all feeling so.

"Good." Jack smiled, pulling out a scrap of paper, a receipt from a sports shop, I saw later, and jotting some notes on it. "Here." He passed it to me. "That's my cell and e-mail. Call me or something." He glanced at Lucas, looking away, arms folded. "When you've got more time."

I tucked it away. "I will." And then, because I had to know, I asked, "So, how's everyone at home?"

"Great," he said. "Been hanging out a lot with the guys from the team. We won States, you know."

"Yeah, I heard. Congrats."

"Thanks."

"And how's Val?" I tried for casual but could tell he saw through me right away. He looked me straight in the eye when he answered.

"We broke up. That wasn't meant for the long haul." He leaned over for a hug. "Be good, Cassie," he whispered.

The warmth of Jack close to me, his tickle of breath on my neck, still made me a little weak, though it shouldn't have. "You too, Jack."

Lucas and I walked back to the car. "A friend from home?" he asked.

"Uh-huh." I replayed the conversation in my mind, wondering if there'd been anything incriminating that Lucas could be angry about. I didn't think so.

He was silent for a few minutes, walking fast, gaining nearly two strides on me. I finally caught up to him near the corner. "This was a bad idea, Cassandra," he said sternly, teacher to student. "It was a mistake for me to encourage it."

Lucas was right about one thing: it was a long drive back to Bering.

chapter 21

There was distance between us after that. A permanent cold front that blew in on our hot summer ride from Wichita. Lucas dropped me off at Drea's, claiming a headache, lots of work to catch up on, plans with friends the next day.

"Where were you?" Drea said before the door even closed behind me. She was sitting at the dining table, papers spread around her open laptop as if she'd been working from home all day. Waiting for me.

I laid my keys on the table by the door. "I went to Wichita with a friend."

"Who?"

"His name's Lucas."

"Well, who is he?' Drea stood, taking a few steps closer and leaning against the wall. "I hope this isn't where you've been spending the night." Her arms were folded across her chest. Nan used to say people did that when they were nervous, protecting themselves. But Drea didn't look nervous.

"Why do you care?"

She frowned. "Because, Cassie, I'm your guardian, remember? It's my right."

"No it isn't, Drea. If you wanted to act like a guardian, you should have started about six weeks ago." Now I was angry. "You've barely talked to me since I've been here, much less asked how I'm spending my time, whether I'm making friends, how I'm feeling about being away from home." I knew my voice had gotten too loud, but at least it kept me from crying. After the day I'd had with Lucas, this was the last thing I needed. "You told me my first day that I'd be on my own. Fine. I've been managing without your help or interest. That's the way *you* wanted it. You can't change the rules now."

"Yes, Cassie," she said evenly. "I can. This is my apartment, not some hotel."

"Funny, because it kind of seemed like one when you pointed to the keys my first day here and said to do 'whatever.'"

Drea just stared at me, then exhaled a long, frustrated sigh. "Okay," she said, and I could tell she was trying hard to stay calm. "Maybe I haven't been as . . . involved as I should have been. I've had a lot going on at work and I wasn't anticipating . . . all this." She waved her hand in my direction. "But we are family, Cassie. I need to make sure you're okay."

"I'm okay."

"I can't let you spend the night with some guy. Especially one I don't even know. For God's sake, Cassie, you're only sixteen."

I thought about mentioning that my mother had been living with a guy—Drea's beloved brother—at my age, but I could see that would just make her angrier and bring us to dangerous ground: her threatening to talk to Lucas or forbid me to see him.

It was time to cut this off. "I'm not," I said. "Lucas is just a friend from school."

Drea's eyes narrowed. Not buying it.

"Really." I rolled my eyes, trying for exasperation. "A philosophy major? *So* not my type. He was going to the city today and asked some of us if we wanted to come along." I shrugged. "I hadn't really seen Wichita and I thought it would be a good chance to check it out."

"Then where *have* you been spending the night?" Unconvinced, but getting there.

"At my friend Becca's. She's in my class too and has a great place near U Park. We study and she's fun to hang out with. Plus, it's easy to get to campus from there." It sounded pretty good and I could see I was making headway. I threw in a guilt trip for good measure. "It's nice to have the company."

Drea smiled a little, her relief visible. Parental duties executed? Check. Okay to get back to my own life? Sure. "Well, okay, Cassie. I'm glad you've found someone you like hanging out with," she said. "I know I'm not around much, but you know if you need me for anything, I'll be there, right?"

"Of course, Drea. Thanks."

"And be careful with this Lucas. Don't forget he's a college guy—they're a lot different from high school boys."

"Don't worry."

I ducked into my room as quickly as I could, telling her it had been a long day. That, at least, was the truth.

I lay on my bed, staring at the unmoving hands of the oversized wall clock, thinking about Lucas, wishing I knew how to fix things. I checked my phone in case I'd missed a call or text from him, though I knew I hadn't.

My philosophy books sat neatly on the nightstand and I reached for one. I couldn't keep my mind on the assignment, though, the sentences blurring together so that I had to read them over and over. I gave up, flipping through the pages and thinking about the class where Lucas had first talked to me, invited me for coffee. My notes from that day littered the margins.

"Who am I?" Professor McMillan had asked. "Defined by values, talents, beliefs," I'd written. Well, I was getting to be a pretty talented liar. First Lucas, now Drea. Of course, if I hadn't told Lucas I was eighteen, we might not be together. I might never have seen the mark on him. Did the end justify the means? I closed my eyes and let the book fall to the side. I didn't want to think about it anymore. None of it. The mark. Lucas. Most of all, me.

I didn't hear from him at all on Friday. Thankfully, I had to work, so I didn't sit home brooding, though every time the door at Cuppa jangled, I glanced up, hopeful. Midway through Saturday I knew I was in that awful limbo where I tried to believe it was classes or friends or absentmindedness that kept him from calling or stopping in at the coffee shop. Since the night we'd gone to dinner, there had rarely been twelve hours we'd been fully apart, not speaking or seeing each other, if even just in class or across the floor of Cuppa. I felt as if I'd done something unspeakably shameful to drive him away so quickly and leave me with so little clue how to reclaim what I needed.

I probably should have let it drop, pretended I'd been joking about the mark or even just let him walk away as he had already started to do, but I couldn't. It was so important to me that Lucas believe. Because if he believed, then he'd know I wasn't crazy and it would all be okay.

I stopped by his apartment after work Tuesday. I still hadn't heard from him. He'd met my eyes briefly after class on Monday, pointing to his watch as he headed for the door, gone before I made it to the front of the room.

The uncertainty of us made me almost physically shaky.

"I have an idea, Lucas." I said after he let me in and I heard his perfunctory excuses about why he hadn't called. "Let's go away this weekend. Really away."

He stared at me, a sheaf of papers still in his hand, making sure I knew he was busy. "What did you have in mind?"

"How about a weekend in the Big Apple?"

"New York City?"

I nodded. "You said you've always wanted to go and so have I. I found a good flight, reasonable too. We could go Friday after you're done with classes, come back late Sunday."

"Don't you have to work?"

"I already talked to Doug and he said it'd be no problem." That wasn't exactly what he'd said, but it was my first request off since I'd started. He wasn't happy about it being a weekend, but how could he refuse? I'd cleared it with Drea too, though she'd been hesitant, said she'd thought maybe we could go shopping or something. Another time, I told her.

I could see Lucas trying to decide and it gave me hope.

"C'mon, Lucas," I said in my best carefree, fun-girl voice. "We'll see a show, the Statue of Liberty, Times Square . . ." Maybe a doomed person or two.

Finally, he relaxed. Even smiled a little. "Yeah, okay, Cassandra. You know what? That's a great idea. Let's do it."

I stayed over that night, and it was almost like it had been before. We read, we talked, we made dinner. I should have left it there, but I was so determined to prove it to him by then that there was no room for other options. Nothing else mattered.

Friday was perfect: cloudless blue skies, Lucas and I holding hands on the airplane. As worldly as he seemed, Lucas had never been to the East Coast and, though normally a little jaded, even he couldn't contain his excitement.

"Look!" he said as we approached. "There's the Statue of Liberty!"

I could just make out a tiny figure on a dot of an island in murky waters. The city itself was like nothing I'd ever imagined, much less seen. Huge buildings rose, seemingly out of the water, impossibly anchored on a narrow strip of land. I'd read that over eight million people lived there, a hundred times the population of Bering. More than enough to find the one I was looking for.

Our Times Square hotel was nothing special, but the surroundings more than made up for it. It was dizzying, the people and cars and lights and the sheer walls of skyscrapers rising everywhere I looked so that it seemed as if I'd fallen to the bottom of a cereal box, closed in on nearly every side. I didn't see anyone with the mark, though if there was ever a time I might have passed one and not noticed, it was then. Lucas and I barely spoke, transfixed by everything happening on the streets outside. It wasn't the awful silence of the prior weekend, but something comfortable, shared.

We had a jam-packed agenda the next day: Liberty Island, Grand Central Terminal, the Empire State Building, Broadway. I don't even remember what else. We started at the TKTS booth in

Times Square, then ventured into the subway, deciphering the map and MetroCard system to get to the Empire State Building. The view from the observation deck was not unlike that which we'd had from the airplane, only this time, we were also balanced precariously on that little strip of land. On top of one of its biggest buildings, no less.

It was hard to grasp the scope of the city—one block equal to the entire downtown of Ashville or Bering. I couldn't imagine how people lived here. Walking the streets, I could pick out the natives by their head-down rush and the almost uniformly focused expression on their faces, everyone wrapped up in their own business, oblivious to everything else.

After the Empire State Building, we went to Grand Central, its massive Great Hall unexpectedly hushed and soothing. Lucas was looking at constellations on the turquoise ceiling while I scanned the crowd. I almost missed her, saw just a flash as she hurried down a side corridor. I grabbed Lucas's arm and started walking fast.

He tried to wiggle free. "Cass! What are you doing?"

"Hurry!" I said. "This way."

"Where are you going?"

I didn't answer, nearly dragging him around the corner where she'd gone. I did a visual sweep, seeing the glow just as she disappeared down an escalator.

I yanked him that way. "C'mon!"

He didn't budge. "What's going on?"

I could tell by his expression that he knew. "I saw one, Lucas. Come with me now or we're going to miss her."

"Cassie..." But I wasn't listening. Nothing mattered but keeping up with her so I could show him.

"Come on!" I ran toward the escalator, not turning to see if he followed.

She was waiting on the train platform. It should have been next to impossible to find one girl among the throngs of people, but the mark made her easy to pick out. Lucas caught up to me, panting a little. "Cassandra . . ."

"Shh. There she is." I led him through the turnstile, onto the platform, keeping her close.

She was young, somewhere around Lucas's age, slightly over-weight, and dressed in slouchy, nondescript black.

The lights of the train crept ominously along the tunnel wall, coming into view shockingly bright and fast. I saw her inch for-ward and, for a second, was sure she was going to jump, but then the cars pounded into the station, stopped, and their doors slid open to dump one wave of people and usher another aboard.

"Let's go." I pulled Lucas with me.

We sat on the opposite side of the car from her. When I was sure she was fully in my sight, I turned to him. He was angry. No matter, I thought. As soon as he saw how this ended, he'd under-stand. Still, I didn't want to fight him the whole way.

"I know you're upset, Lucas," I said, "but this is a chance to see . . ." He wasn't listening, couldn't hear me past his anger. I tried to find something that would resonate with him. "Think of it as testing a hypothesis. Right now, you think I'm off my rocker. Humor me. Test your theory to see if you're right or if, maybe, there's actually something to what I'm telling you."

"This isn't how I thought we were going to spend our day," he said petulantly.

"Me either," I lied.

The train swayed bumpily, jostling passengers, forcing us to dance to the same beat while it clattered through the tight dark tunnels. I studied the girl, trying to read her, to see if she had any inkling that today was somehow different. I always wonder that. Do they realize that this is the last day they will buy a newspaper at that stand, pay cab fare, kiss their wife or kids? They seem as harried and haggard and unappreciative of each action—though it will be their last—as everyone else. In contrast, I've started to feel everything acutely, overaware of stepping off the curb, turning a page, drinking my coffee, savoring every sensation, not knowing whether, if it were my last day, I would see the light framing my reflected image.

I think about death more than most people, I'm sure, the mark never letting me forget how unexpectedly it can happen. Like the girl whose day is today. Her skin is slack and pasty, so maybe she's sick. But if she were terminal, it's hard to imagine she could be out, walking around. Most likely, it will be an accident.

The train rumbled into another stop and she stood.

I nudged Lucas. "Let's go."

She trudged through the dirty station, past the tiled sign that read BOWERY, and up the stairs to the dirtier street outside. The buildings were smaller here and I winced at the sunlight, sharp and startling after the subway's dimness. I kept us about a block behind, trailing her safely across three intersections. Midway down the last block, she stopped at a door, rummaged in her bag for a key, and disappeared inside. I tried the knob when we got there, but it was locked tight.

"Now what?" Lucas demanded, hands on his hips.

I scanned the names by the buzzer, about ten in all, trying to figure out which might be hers and whether I could somehow get her to invite us in. Even in Bering, though, you wouldn't spend a day with total strangers. Here, you didn't even look at them.

"I guess we wait."

"For what?"

"For her to come back out."

"That's ridiculous, Cassandra. This whole thing is ridiculous." Lucas exhaled through pursed lips.

"We could get some lunch, maybe," I suggested, pointing across the street. "Look. There's a café right there."

Lucas glanced over, studying the people lounging at the metal tables packed tightly on the sidewalk out front. "Listen," he said, and I could already read his answer in that one disappointed word. "I came to New York to see the city, not to follow some hapless girl around. I'm going to the Statue of Liberty. If you want to come, I'd love to have you, but I'm tired of this, Cass. I really don't want to hear anything else about this . . . whatever it is you think you can do or see . . ."

He kept talking, but I noticed the people at the café, couple by couple, had paused to look our way. Not at us, exactly, but up. I turned to see what they were looking at.

"Lucas," was all I said.

"What?"

But I didn't answer, couldn't, because I knew this was it. He followed my gaze to the top of the six-story brown building in front of us. I could just see her as she stood at the edge of the roof. Instinctively, I stepped back, pulling Lucas with me.

Her fall was a horrible, silent drop.

The first thing Lucas did was throw up. Around us, people were screaming. There was pandemonium just like Mr. McKenzie's accident, people running out of the restaurant, to the scene or away, some just standing there stunned. I had turned my head just before she hit, knowing already how a sight like that can linger in your memory for . . . well, forever. The sound was bad enough, repeating in my brain over and over as I dragged Lucas, ashen and shaking, around the corner, out of sight.

Slowly I led him to a stoop about halfway down the block. He was still heaving as we sat. "The police are coming," he said as the wail of sirens came closer.

"Probably. Or it might be an ambulance."

"She couldn't have survived, could she?"

I shook my head.

"The police will want to talk to us," he said shakily. "We're witnesses."

"There were plenty of witnesses there, Lucas. We didn't see anything more than they did. Nothing we can talk about, at least." I felt eerily calm. Was I becoming numb to death? But then I remembered the sound, that awful crunching thud. I wasn't shaken up the way Lucas was, but I'd known what was coming and maybe having him with me—someone else who'd seen, who'd understand—was making it easier or more bearable, though it really wasn't either. I felt helpless and horribly, horribly sad. It was impossible to imagine things being bad enough to do what she had just done.

Lucas looked at me sideways, from the corners of his eyes, as if afraid to face me full-on. "How did you know?" he whispered.

"I told you. She had the mark."

He nodded, looking away, down the busy street, where cars streamed by, passengers giggling, talking, unaware that someone had just taken her own life steps away.

"Let's get out of here," I suggested.

I hailed a cab. "Central Park," I told the driver. I'd never been there, but I hoped it was as tranquil as the green spaces in Bering.

We were silent on the ride past more buildings, streets, stores, people. I closed my eyes, not wanting to see another. The driver dropped us at a corner with horse-drawn carriages. "Can't go in," he said shortly. "Roads are closed on the weekend."

I paid him and we entered the park, walking a curved lane until we came to a field. We sat somewhere in the middle, the sun full on us for the first time that day. Neither of us spoke. I studied the buildings rising like giants above the trees beyond.

"You really can . . . see something . . ." Lucas finally said.

"Yes, I can."

"I didn't believe you."

"I know."

"I mean . . ." He shook his head. "I can't believe what we just saw. I don't think I'll ever get that out of my mind. The way she fell . . ."

He wouldn't, but I didn't want to tell him that.

"You've seen that . . . that kind of thing before?" he asked.

"Not exactly, but something like it. I saw a man hit by a car."

He winced. "That must have been awful."

"It was."

"How can you . . ."

"It's not always like that, Lucas. Most of the time, I don't actu-ally see them die. I just see the mark."

"What is it? What does it look like?"

I described it the best I could, none of my images exactly right.

"How long has this been happening?"

"Forever." I told him about the schoolkids, random people I'd seen. "I didn't really figure it out until my grandmother was in the hospital and I saw it on her roommate. When I went back to visit the next day, the roommate was gone. Passed away. I started thinking about it, putting the pieces together. The next time I saw it, I did what we just did. Followed a man until . . . it ended. That was the car accident."

Lucas was calmer, the color back in his cheeks and, with each question, he sounded steadier. In front of us, a trio of guys threw a football. Their shirts were off and, unlike the girl we'd followed, they seemed the picture of health, toned and laughing. I watched them for a while, until Lucas said softly, "You really saw it on me?"

I glanced over and, for the first time today, saw him actually looking at me. Not annoyed, not dismissive, a penetrating stare. "I did."

"And then it went away?"

"It did."

"Do you think I was meant to die that day?"

"I think something would have happened if you had gone out. Something bad. That's what the mark means."

"You saved my life, didn't you?"

I shrugged. "I don't know, Lucas. That's never happened before."

We watched the football players a little longer. They reminded me of the picture in Lucas's apartment of him with his high school friends. Maybe he thought so too.

"I don't want to stay here anymore," he said.

I nodded. "You want to go back to the hotel?"

"No. I don't want to stay in this city. I want to go home."

"Our flight back isn't until tomorrow."

He shook his head. "Let's change it." He stood. "Let's pack and go to the airport."

"Don't you think we should call first? See if there's anything available? Or what it'll cost?"

"I don't care. We can fly standby. Even if we have to sleep in the airport, it'll be better than staying here."

I didn't argue with him, didn't blame him for wanting to get away from what he'd seen.

chapter 22

We made it back to Bering late that night, well past midnight. Lucas dropped me at the apartment. I was disappointed. It felt like a replay of our last drive back from Wichita.

"You understand, Cassandra," he said. "It's been a very long day. I just need . . . I don't know . . . some time."

I nodded, but I didn't understand. I had proved I wasn't crazy, hadn't I? "I know this is hard to absorb, Lucas," I said. "Maybe I can help. I've had some experience with this—"

He cut me off with a curt shake of his head. "Thanks, but I think I need to just . . . work through this myself, you know?"

"Sure."

"I'll call you."

"You're back early," Drea said. "What happened?"

"Becca got sick," I told her.

I waited. A day passed. Then two, then three. I slept, I worked,

I read three books. I watched the phone. I'd been sure I'd catch him in class Monday, but he came late and left early, avoiding my eyes the whole time.

"You and your boyfriend break up?" Doug asked.

"No, why?"

"I don't know. I haven't seen him around much."

I shrugged. "He's busy with classes, papers, you know."

"Uh-huh."

Finally, on Wednesday, he called. "Let's have lunch," he said. "I want to talk to you."

He was already at Café Lennox when I arrived. He waved me over but didn't stand, didn't offer a hug or kiss. We're on campus, I told myself. He has to be careful here.

He didn't waste time on preliminaries. "I've been thinking," he said after I returned to the table with my food, "about your gift."

I hadn't thought of it like that, couldn't quite agree, but I didn't argue.

"Tell me more about it."

"What do you want to know?"

"You said you've seen it forever."

"Right."

"And you figured out what it meant when? Six months ago?"

"About that. A little less."

"But you kind of already knew, right? When you followed the man who got hit by a car."

"Kind of. Not really."

Lucas nodded. His questions had a rhythm, like they did in class when he was leading more than exploring, taking me to a destination he had already chosen. "How often have you seen it since?"

"I don't know. A few times. More here than I did in Ashville."

"Have you ever told anyone? Tried to warn them?"

"Only you."

He nodded again, leaning back and watching me closely. "Didn't it ever occur to you to try to stop it, Cassandra? To help them?"

We had arrived and it wasn't where I wanted to be. Not at all. I had proved I wasn't crazy. Things were supposed to go back to normal, the way they'd been—us reading together on his couch, taking walks, sharing dinner. "No, not really," I answered. "I . . . I mean, how could I think I could stop it?"

"You thought you could with me."

"I didn't really, Lucas. I just . . . I couldn't *not* say something. I didn't really think I could change anything."

"You must have. Or you wouldn't have told me to stay home. What did you think you were doing if you weren't trying to change things?"

"Why are you attacking me?"

"I'm not attacking, Cassie. I'm just trying to understand how you could see this mark on all those people—mothers, fathers, kids, for crissake—and not try to do something about it. Why wouldn't you?"

"Would you?"

"Of course. I'd feel it was my duty."

"Your duty?!"

"Yes. Just like we talked about in class, at dinner. Your 'hypo-thetical,' except that it isn't about letting someone decide how to use their remaining time; it's about giving them more time. Saving lives. Jesus, Cassie, how could you not try to help?"

"Look," I said, feeling my face start to burn, "the truth is I had already tried and it didn't work. The day Nan died. I saw it on her, the doctors ran all kinds of tests. But how could they know? It could have been anything. If I couldn't stop it for her, with so many people trying, how could I stop it for anyone else?"

Lucas stared at me, frowning. "That's it, Cassandra? One time? You tried once and gave up?"

"I didn't give up," I said defensively. "Besides, even if I'd thought I could change things, who says I'm supposed to? What if it's not the right thing to do?"

"Right for them or for you?"

"Are you calling me selfish?" My tone told him I was outraged, but really I was as angry and frustrated with myself as I was with Lucas. His interrogation was bringing up all the things I'd been struggling with these many months. Things I'd wondered about, but did nothing, not nearly enough, I thought now, to explore.

"I'm just wondering, Cassandra. I don't understand your objection. You have the power to save lives." He asked again, "Why wouldn't you?"

The way Lucas said it, it seemed so simple. Why wouldn't I?

It was then that it struck me—I had let that girl die. I'd known I might change things, had done so for Lucas, but had chosen to stay silent, following her down those dirty New York sidewalks to her fated destination. Watching as she jumped. I felt monstrous. Is *this* who I am?

Still, something held me back from wanting to dive headlong into rescuing everyone marked by the light. What about what was meant to be? Fate? In my gut, I knew there was more. Had to be, or I was just a coward. Or worse. "What if I'm not supposed to tell?"

"What do you mean?"

"What if . . . this mark . . . is really meant just for me to see?"

"Why would it be? Meant for you by whom?"

"I don't know. God?"

"Ridiculous," Lucas said. "Do you think God would give you an ability you weren't meant to use? Is a gifted pianist meant not to play? An artist not to paint? It doesn't make sense, Cassandra."

"So I'm to save these people? God put me here, with this ability, to hold off death for the people of Bering, Kansas? Does that make sense, Lucas?"

He shrugged.

"And what, might I ask, would you say? Hi, I'm Lucas and today's your day to die?"

"I'm not in your shoes, Cassie, so I'm sure it's easy for me to say," Lucas said quietly, "but I'd like to think I'd figure something out."

I stared at my food angrily. *How dare he.*

"Listen." Lucas leaned in, speaking softly. "I know it's hard, but don't you think you should at least consider it?"

"What could I have done for that girl, Lucas? She already knew it was her day to die."

He nodded. "I thought about that. But maybe if you had talked to her, you'd have realized the problem, could have told someone else."

I snorted. "Right. In a five-minute conversation I could have deduced that she was suicidal."

"Well, don't forget, you had a head start. You knew she was going to die. Surely you considered that possibility?"

I remembered the train rushing into the station, thinking she might jump. I said nothing.

"Maybe nothing would have come of it," Lucas acknowledged. "Maybe you wouldn't have figured it out. But maybe you would."

"And if I had, then what? If I knew her, maybe I could have helped, reminded her that people cared or that things'll get better, but honestly, Lucas, why would she believe a total stranger? Why would she even stop to listen?"

He shrugged. "Maybe she wouldn't have, but you don't know. Maybe just talking to her about death would have scared her enough to make her reconsider, Cassie." He continued, "What you do know is that it couldn't be any worse, right? I mean, she was already going to die. Anything would be worth trying, wouldn't it?"

It was hard to disagree, but I wasn't ready to agree either.

"Think about what you're saying, Lucas," I countered. "What would that mean for me? Following people around, trying to convince them they're about to die? They'd never believe me. Think about how you reacted. You thought I was nuts, and you know me."

"But I listened," he said, "and I'm still here."

I was silent.

"It won't be easy, Cassandra. You're right about that. But you're strong. It's one of the things I admired about you, what drew me to you. I would never have pegged you as one to take the easy way out. Especially about something as important as this. Don't you see?" he said earnestly. "This is it. Your purpose. Maybe mine too. Helping you use this extraordinary gift."

I knew then that this was more than a conversation. It was an ultimatum. And maybe he was right. Maybe it was as simple as helping people and I was taking the coward's way out. "All right, Lucas," I mumbled, struggling to say the words. "I'll try."

He beamed. "You're making the right decision, Cassandra. And I will support you a hundred percent. I want you to tell me all about it: who you see, what you say to them, how they react . . ." He rambled on, about how incredible this was, about destiny and meaning. I stopped listening, already dreading the days ahead, actually doing what I'd just agreed to.

Finally Lucas stood, collecting our trays, smiling at me. "We'll do it together, Cassandra. Together we'll find a way to turn this into the best possible good."

I stayed with him that night. I should have been thrilled, but there was something different in the way he looked at me. I used to catch him watching as I read or dressed or cooked, but his expression now was as if he were watching a rare but dangerous animal: intrigued, drawn, repelled, and above all, cautious. He smiled when I caught him looking, but it was without warmth. Calculating.

"Remember," he said the next day as we were leaving the apartment, "if you see one, you can call me. I'll come help you or if I'm too far, we can talk through what you should say. I'll keep my cell on vibrate during meetings. I'll see you in class."

I hadn't studied for that day's lesson, only skimmed the reading. It was the first time I'd slacked, but with all that had happened, I just couldn't do it.

After class, I barely had time to collect my books before he was at my side. "Did you see anything?" he whispered urgently.

I shook my head.

"I've got the afternoon free," he said. "Let's go look. We can go to the mall or in town to the square . . ."

"I can't, Lucas," I lied. "I promised Doug I'd help him with some stuff at the shop."

"I thought you were off today."

I shrugged. "We got some extra orders; he asked if I could help with restocking, inventory, you know."

"What time will you be finished?"

I had to squeeze past him to get through the door. "Not sure," I said. "I'll call you."

chapter 23

He wanted to be with me all the time. I was less a girlfriend than a project. Every conversation started with: "Did you see one yet?" He was disappointed when I said no, but he would have been equally disappointed if I'd said yes and failed to call him before the confrontation.

At Lucas's behest, I'd been spending my free time haunting the most populated places of Bering: the town square, the shopping centers, even the strip of bars near campus at night. Lucas came with me for those excursions. In all our times out, I'd seen nothing, but I developed a persistent stomachache, my gut churning unpleasantly every morning at the thought of another day searching.

Finally I decided to give myself a day off. It was a Tuesday, Lucas's busiest day on campus, so I knew he'd be less likely to hound me and I had the early shift at Cuppa, with the rest of the day free. It was mid-August, still hot, but breezy, and I was determined to spend it away from the places I'd been visiting in search of the mark. I planned to read by my pond in the park, not for class, but purely for pleasure, something that felt in very short supply lately.

I was walking down the path toward the pond when I saw a woman pushing a stroller. As she came closer, what I first suspected was confirmed: there was a misty glow inside the hooded carriage, a mark on her baby. I slowed down, not wanting the moment to come when our paths would cross and I either would or wouldn't do as I'd promised.

This was exactly the kind of untimely death that should be prevented, I thought, gritting my teeth. My mind raced, working through the things I could say, but she was nearly upon me and I was so nervous that I knew I wouldn't be able to stammer anything coherent. She smiled pleasantly. I glanced inside the stroller. The baby was small. An infant, wrapped in a blanket monogrammed JDS, sleeping peacefully amid a pool of light. And then she was past.

"Excuse me," I said, too loudly.

She turned back. "Yes?"

"I . . . I . . ."

She looked concerned. "Are you okay? Do you need help?"

I shook my head. "I . . . This is going to sound crazy," I said hoarsely, "but I think something's going to happen to your baby."

She drew back sharply, as if I'd threatened her. "What are you talking about?"

I held out my hands, trying to soothe. "I don't mean to scare you. I . . . I'm a little bit psychic. I can see things sometimes . . ." She was backing up, angry and afraid.

"Stay away," she said shrilly, looking around for help. "Don't get near me."

"No, no, I won't." This was going terribly. I had done it all wrong. She wasn't even listening. "I'm just trying to help, to warn you. I think your baby might be in danger. Has . . ." I looked back at the stroller, trying to get the gender right, but she had turned it fully away and was standing in front, blocking my view. "Has he or she been sick?"

Her voice was low, barely controlled. "If you say one more word to me, I'm going to scream and then call the police. Do you understand?"

I nodded.

"There is nothing wrong with my baby, but there's something *seriously* wrong with you. Get the hell away from me." With that, she turned and practically ran out of the park, the stroller jouncing along in front.

I sat on the grass, shaking as I fumbled for my phone.

"Hello?" Lucas whispered.

"It's me. I saw one."

"Hold on." He was back on the line thirty seconds later. "I left my meeting. Tell me about it, Cassandra. Is the person still there?"

"No. She left."

"Did you talk to her?"

"I tried. It . . . it was a mess." I started crying.

"Oh, Cassie, I'm sorry. Where are you? I'll come get you."

"No, no, it's okay." I wiped at the tears and took a deep breath. "It was a woman. With a baby. The baby had the mark."

"Oh."

"Yeah. I tried, Lucas. I really did, but I guess I didn't do it right, because she didn't listen, she got scared and pissed . . ."

"Tell me what happened."

So I did. When I was finished, he said, "I'm proud of you for trying, Cassandra. I know it wasn't easy. Who knows? Maybe she did hear you. Maybe she'll think about what you said later, when she calms down."

That made me feel a little better. "Maybe."

But she didn't. Or, if she did, she wasn't able to protect the baby anyway. We found his obituary two days later. Jacob Daniel Stern, four months old. Crib death.

Lucas left for school, but I stayed in his apartment, unable to drag myself through the routines that would get me to work on time. Did she think of me when she found her baby that morning? What had I done but compound her guilt about something she had little, maybe no control over? I wanted to bang my head on the table or scream my guts out. It was so unfair.

Lucas tried to cheer me up that night, but I could tell he felt it too. There is nothing poetic about death. It is ugly and awful, and the more time you spend around it, the uglier and more awful you feel.

"You've got to keep at it, Cassandra," he told me in his "buck up, little camper" speech. "You tried. It's not like you made anything worse. It was going to happen anyway."

I was too exhausted and depressed to argue or tell him that I probably *had* made it worse. I had stayed in bed all day. Lucas brought me soup and tea for dinner and didn't even try to make me get up.

I skipped class that week, called in to work too. I moped around Drea's apartment during the times I wasn't at Lucas's. Drea had gotten over her brief bout of guilt or responsibility, whatever it had been, and was back to her usual absent self. They'd won a new client, she'd told me, were totally immersed.

Finally, by the weekend, I decided it was time to put it aside. Being at Cuppa helped. I dug back into my philosophy lessons too, anything to take my mind off what had happened.

On Sunday, five days after my day in the park, Lucas asked gently if I didn't think I should try again.

"You know, get back out there, see if you can find another that you might be able to help."

"I don't think I can do it, Lucas."

"Wouldn't it help if it worked? Erase the sting of . . . of this last one?"

"And what if it didn't? You saw how hard this was." I shook my head. "I don't think I'm cut out for this."

"Cassandra, you're the only one cut out for this. Who else has the ability? You're stronger than you know. It's hard, but . . ." I stopped listening, knowing how the speech went, having heard a hundred iterations of it already.

"Fine, fine," I said, holding up my hands, anything to stop the barrage of words.

I could have just lied to Lucas, told him I didn't see any. After all, more often than not, it had been months, even years between times I saw the mark. The truth is, as much as I dreaded having to talk to another one, I did wonder if Lucas was right. I mean, there had to be a reason I could see the mark, didn't there? One attempt was hardly a fair test.

I read the coroner's statistics: one hundred seventy-some accidental deaths a year in a population of over eighty thousand. I tried to figure out how many people I saw each day. Working at Cuppa alone—between customers and those who passed our window—the number had to be in the hundreds. Realizing that made me feel better, helped explain why I'd seen more here than in Ashville. Then, if I added making the rounds, as I'd come to call it—visiting downtown, the malls, the parks—I had to be hitting the thousands. It wasn't like I needed to be close to the person. The light made them stand out, even in a crowd, like the girl in New York.

I didn't want to live with the idea of myself as a coward. So I gutted it out and went back to looking.

I saw him from two blocks away, sitting by the skeleton of a building. He was a construction worker, his yellow hat on the bench beside him, next to a steaming cup of coffee and a white wrapper holding half a sub.

I strode right up to him, determined to get it out before I lost my nerve.

"Jes?" His voice was warm, but heavily accented.

"I'm going to tell you something that will sound strange," I said calmly. "I'm a little psychic, sometimes I can see things."

He had stopped eating, staring at me expressionlessly. For a minute I thought maybe he didn't speak English.

"Do you understand?" I asked slowly.

He nodded, his eyes wary.

"I think you're in danger," I told him.

"*Dios mio,*" he muttered, crossing himself.

"I don't know what you have planned today, but if you can, go home and stay there. Don't go back to work or drive your car or . . ."

He was gathering his things, knocking his hat clumsily off the bench. I bent to pick it up for him, but he snatched it away before I could touch it. He glanced back at me, his eyes wide, his right hand fluttering, repeating the sign of the cross, I realized.

"I'm sorry," I said, but he was already backing away. Then he turned and ran.

"Is he there?"

I had told Lucas about the construction worker when I got to his apartment the night before. He said I did a great job, that it sounded like it had gone better. I guessed it had. He hadn't threatened me with the police or started screaming, though that seemed a pretty low bar for success.

Reluctantly I scanned the obits that Lucas had dropped in front of me first thing in the morning. I felt a jolt of elation. There was no one under sixty.

Lucas saw my expression. "That's what I thought," he said, smiling. "You did it."

"Let's not celebrate yet," I warned. "Maybe something happened later, after the paper went to print." But he wasn't in the next day's either. I felt sure he was local, that it wasn't an accident on the road, something that wouldn't make the *Bering News*.

Lucas took me to dinner at Gianna's the day after, the paper still absent news of the worker. Over champagne, he asked, "How do you feel?"

"Honestly, I'm still trying to digest it, Lucas. It's hard to believe that it worked."

"Why? It worked with me."

"Yeah, it's just that . . . well, it's a lot to absorb."

He nodded. "It's just like I told you, Cassandra. There is a purpose to your gift. You can save lives."

"I guess the key is getting them to listen," I said, sounding more reasoned than I felt. The idea that something I did or said had that kind of power was overwhelming.

He nodded. "That's right. And you'll get better and better at it over time. There will always be people who don't heed your warning, but doesn't it feel great to have saved someone who did?"

"Yeah," I said, smiling. "Yeah, I guess it does."

chapter 24

It was three days later that I saw him again. This time, on the front page of the paper. My first thought was that you can't cheat death after all. Then I realized he was in handcuffs.

I pulled the folded sheets out of the newsstand rack to read the caption:

EDUARD SANCHEZ, 39, IS LED FROM HIS
APARTMENT BUILDING WHERE POLICE
RESPONDING TO A 911 CALL FOUND HIS
WIFE, STABBED FIVE TIMES.

"You gonna buy that or not?"

I gave the newsie a buck and walked away skimming the article. Multiple domestic disputes, fired from his job the day before, no children or nearby relatives.

I found myself at the edge of the park, five blocks from Cuppa, where I was due in three minutes. I pulled out my phone.

"Doug? It's Cassie," I said when he answered breathlessly. "I'm so sorry for the short notice, but I'm not going to make it in today."

He hesitated. I think I'd called in more times in the last few weeks than I'd showed up. "What's wrong?" he asked finally. "Are you okay?"

"Yeah, I'm just . . . not feeling good. I was on my way in, but I don't think I can do it."

Mechanically I entered the park and found a bench near the pond, deliberately facing away from the fields and paths, unable to bear the thought of people. I still held the paper but couldn't bring myself to look at the article again. He'd stabbed his wife. Maybe upset about losing his job, one I'd sent him running from. Damned if you do, damned if you don't.

I needed someone to talk to, but Lucas was no good. He was becoming zealous, always talking about our purpose. He was the last person who could help me sort it out.

Briefly I thought of Drea. No. Impossible.

There was no one who knew and no one I could tell, not after the way these past weeks had gone. If only Nan were still here, I thought, and then suddenly realized exactly where I should go. They say dead men tell no tales. I decided to give it a try. Maybe they were the perfect ones to listen.

I found them at the second cemetery I went to. A single headstone with a single word: RENFIELD.

"Hi guys," I whispered. I sat on the grass beside the marker, curling my legs tight to my chest. The cemetery around me was deserted.

"I'm sorry it took me so long to come," I said to the smooth gray marble. "I've been meaning to. I've thought about you a lot since I've been here. It's a great town, Bering. I bet it would have been a great place to grow up."

It was easy to picture: a farmhouse in the sunflower fields I had passed on my ride from the airport back in May or one of the trim brownstones near school.

"I came today because I need help," I said softly. "If you've been watching me—and I've always thought that you do—you know about the mark. It's an awful thing. Or maybe . . . maybe it's a good thing and I just don't know how to use it." I sighed. "But I don't know what to do. The thing is that it looks like I really can warn people, maybe prevent their death, but I can't tell if I *should*. I mean, Lucas is still here and that's a good thing, but he and I are a mess. So I guess I saved him but ruined our relationship." I took a breath, realizing how much it hurt to admit that he and I were over. Even though I kept going to his apartment, executing the motions, I knew it was only a matter of time.

"Not that a relationship is worth even close to as much as a life. He's young and smart. It had to be a good thing to save him.

"But last week," I said, "I warned the wrong kind of guy. I saved him and he killed his wife. I don't know how I could have known. He was young too. It seemed like the right thing . . ."

I shivered, a chill running down my spine. "Lucas makes it sound so logical—if I can save lives, why wouldn't I—but I just don't know if these lives are meant to be saved. What if it's truly their time?"

It always came back to that—my gut instinct that fate wasn't meant to be tampered with. All around me, marked by these headstones, were people whose time had come. Life had gone on for those around them—for me, when my own parents had gone—and my time with Nan had been good, maybe the way it was meant to be.

"Anyway," I said finally, "I know you can't tell me what to do. Even if you were here you wouldn't be able to, but thanks for listening. Mom. Dad."

Their names, spoken aloud, sounded weird and wistful. I'd never said them before.

I stood, stretched, felt better. I didn't have any answers, but it's funny how talking to someone, even if that someone is mostly yourself, is cathartic.

I'm not sure what made me do it, maybe the feeling that it was odd there were no names or dates on the stone, but I circled the marker and sure enough, there they were. First my grandparents—Samuel and Paula—and the start and end dates of their lives, such a brief summary. Then, below them, my parents: Daniel and Georgia. I squatted, tracing the letters with my finger, trying to remember anything about them, not things I'd been told, but things I'd experienced. Of course, it was all too far back.

Then my eyes shifted to the dates. I had to look twice to be sure I was reading them right, that the elements or vandals hadn't changed them, but they were crisp and clear as if they'd been carved yesterday.

And they were wrong. According to the headstone, my mother died four years after my father.

chapter 25

I sat in the apartment, still and quiet. I'd wanted to see Drea. When she didn't answer my voice mail, I texted her. Twice. "When r u coming home?" I wrote. "Need to talk." She wasn't, she finally responded, had been called away on business, could it wait? I didn't answer, not sure if it could, not sure if she'd have the answers to my questions anyway.

I didn't return Lucas's calls either, his voice on my messages increasingly frantic. "I'm worried about you, Cassandra. Did something happen? Did you see one? Call me."

After Cuppa closed, I left a message on the machine. "Hi, Doug, it's Cassie. I'm sorry, but I'm not going to make it in again tomorrow. In fact, I'm probably going to need some time. A few days at least. I know I've been out a lot, but I've got some stuff going on. Nothing major, just things I have to take care of. I understand if you have to fire me. Just . . . let me know, I guess."

I waited for the day to end and for the sleeping pill I'd taken, one last one, left over from after Nan's death, to take effect.

I couldn't understand why Nan had lied to me. In all the time I'd known her, there wasn't another thing I could remember her lying about. Nothing. Not stupid things like how I looked in a certain dress or important ones like whether she'd loved her husband. There were things she just didn't talk about, but this was different. Why would she make me believe my mother had died in a car crash along with my father, if that's even how he died? What else had she lied about?

I was waiting at the door when the Bering Library opened the next morning. Despite the new building, they were as slow to transition to the digital age as Ashville had been.

"The dates you're looking for would be on microfilm," the librarian, a nattily dressed man, told me.

"In the basement?"

He laughed. "No, we won't send you to the dungeon. It's right over here." He led me to a small, glass-enclosed room housing two of the large viewing machines. "Now, what did you want to start with?"

I gave him the date under my father's name on the headstone. I figured I'd start with the car accident or whatever it was and work forward from there.

The librarian brought me two yellowed boxes. "The week's papers start with Sunday the third, so what you're looking for should be right at the beginning, but I brought it all anyway. Do you know how to work this machine?"

It looked just like the ones in Ashville. I nodded, but he proceeded to tell me anyway. I didn't interrupt, willing to postpone what I was about to read for another few minutes.

When he left, I threaded the dark film into the viewer and

pulled up the first page. I expected it would be the headline article, but there was nothing. I scrolled through all of Sunday, just to be sure, then moved on to the Monday edition. Sure enough, it was the lead story:

LENNOX PROFESSOR KILLED
IN THREE-CAR ACCIDENT

Daniel Renfield, 38, of Chestnut Street in Bering, was pronounced dead at the scene of a traffic accident Sunday afternoon. Two passengers, his wife, Georgia Renfield, 30, and the couple's young daughter, Cassandra, were taken to Metro-West Medical Center for treatment.

The car, a Chrysler sedan, was reportedly hit from behind and pushed into oncoming traffic. Bystanders said that Mr. Renfield, a professor at nearby Lennox University, was stopped at a traffic light when his car was rear-ended into an intersection and hit by a white delivery van.

The accident will be the subject of continuing investigation by the Bering Police Department and the Office of the Chief Medical Examiner.

The car was a gruesome, mangled mess, the driver's side completely mashed in, the windshield splintered outward from a clear impact above where the steering wheel would have been. I had never considered that I was in the car with them, but of course I was. Where else would I have been?

I scrolled through the next couple days, looking for more: the results of the investigation, reports on my mother's condition and mine. There was a brief snippet about my being released to Nan's custody and, a day later, my mother was released. That same day, my father's obituary was printed:

RENFIELD, DANIEL

Daniel Renfield, 38, died on Sunday, April 3, in a traffic accident.

Born at Wilcox Memorial Hospital, Daniel graduated from Bering High and earned a BA at the University of Pennsylvania. He returned to Kansas to complete his doctorate in ancient history at Wichita State. He began as an instructor at Lennox University the following year.

Daniel is survived by his parents, Samuel and Paula, of Bering, one sister, Andrea Soto of Atlanta, his wife of 10 years, Georgia, and his 2-year-old daughter, Cassandra.

The funeral service will be held Friday, April 8, at 11 a.m. at Community Unitarian Church, Maple Avenue.

That was it. I got the librarian to fetch another two weeks' worth of film, but there wasn't another mention of it. My father's death faded away, replaced by news of the annual Easter parade and debate over new road construction.

It was what I had expected, the story I'd always been told. Except that my mother and I both survived, left the scene together, but for some reason, hadn't remained that way.

"All finished?" the librarian asked as I approached his circular desk.

"I'm finished with those films. I was hoping to see another date."

He nodded. "Why don't you give me all the dates you're looking for and I can pull them all at once. I can't leave the desk too often."

I glanced around the deserted library. "Um, okay. I think this is the only one." I handed him the date of my mother's death. "But maybe pull the week before and week after."

I started with February 5, the date on her headstone, a little less than four years after the car accident. Nothing. I checked the sixth, then the seventh. Still nothing. I wondered if maybe there *was* some mistake. The grave actually was wrong or I'd somehow misread it. Then on the eighth I found it.

RENFIELD, GEORGIA

Georgia Renfield, 34, died suddenly Tuesday evening. The cause of death was not immediately released.

Ms. Renfield, a resident of the Joan Barrow Center in Ridgevale, previously lived with her husband, Daniel, a Lennox University professor who was killed in a car accident.

Ms. Renfield is survived by a 6-year-old daughter, Cassandra, and her mother, Nanette Dinakis, both of Ashville, Pennsylvania.

Funeral services will be held today at Community Unitarian Church, Maple Avenue.

"More dates?" the librarian asked as I approached.

"No." I handed him the boxes. "I'm all set." He started to skirt the desk to return them to their appropriate homes. "Do you know what the Joan Barrow Center is?"

He paused. "I do. It's a mental health hospital. I think it's in Norton or Martinville."

"Ridgevale."

He shrugged. "Yeah, okay, they're all pretty close. About an hour south of here."

The pieces were coming together: why I'd been with Nan when my mother was still alive, why Nan hadn't told me the truth, though I still thought she should have.

"Do you know how to get there?"

"I do." He went back behind his counter and rummaged underneath. He pulled out a map. "You go . . ."

I stopped him. "I don't have a car. Is there public transportation? A bus or anything?"

"I doubt it," he said. "It's not exactly a popular destination."

I thought about asking Lucas to borrow his car. He'd probably let me, but I couldn't bear the thought of all his questions and prodding. It would be an expensive ride, but a cab seemed my only option.

I was nervous on the ride there, a little about what I'd find, but more that I wouldn't be able to fill in the blanks. I had no idea what the laws were. Was I privy to my mother's medical records? Would they even have something from so long ago still on file? I felt sure that, at some point, I'd learn whatever secrets the Joan Barrow Center held, but I didn't want to wait for some point. I needed to see them now. Today.

"You want me to wait?" the cabbie asked when we pulled up to the front steps, his tires crunching on gravel.

I did, but I didn't know if it'd be five minutes or five hours. I decided to be optimistic. "Nah, that's okay. Thanks."

He nodded, took the fifty I gave him, and rolled slowly down the long drive. I had expected either a country club or institution, but the Joan Barrow Center was neither. The fenced grounds were pleasant, but not so secluded that neighboring homes were hidden. The main building, where I now ascended three cement steps, was flanked by two smaller ones, all of them brick. I could see more of the same construction—sturdy and sensible—scattered along cement walkways. I entered through the double wooden doors into a bright and clean foyer with a reception desk squarely in its middle.

"May I help you?" The woman looked as sturdy and sensible as the buildings, neither welcoming nor unfriendly.

I tried to be as warm as the hollowness in my gut would allow. "I'm hoping to look at some records. Of a patient. My mother. She was here about ten years ago."

The woman frowned. "Do you have an appointment?"

"No."

She shook her head. "I'm sorry, but you need an appointment."

Just what I was afraid of. "I'm . . . Is there someone, one of the doctors maybe that I could talk to? Just for a minute?" She was already shaking her head. I decided to go for broke. "I've come a long way. I took a taxi all the way from Bering and—"

"You should have called first. I could have saved you the trouble."

I nodded. "I know. I probably should have. It's just . . . I just learned that my mother was here the last years of her life. She died when I was two. Well, that's what I'd always thought, but then I learned today that she didn't. She just . . . came here. I really need to learn her story. You can understand that, can't you?"

She kept frowning, so I kept talking. "I know maybe I can't see her records today, but maybe, if I could just talk to one of the doctors, understand the procedures . . ."

She held up a hand. "Okay. I can't promise anything, but I'll call Dr. Gordon."

I recognized her as soon as she walked through the door, even without her boots and eyeliner. Her hair was dark brown, still not her natural color, I thought, but softer than black. She paused when she saw me, touched her finger to her mouth, then snapped and shook it speculatively at me as she approached.

"I know you."

I nodded.

"Wait. Don't tell me." She smiled triumphantly. "The girl on the plane. Helen."

"Cassandra," I corrected.

"Riiight." She turned back to the receptionist. "Thanks, Beth, I'll take it from here." She motioned me to the stairs behind the desk. "Come to my office." I followed her up the curved staircase.

"So," she said as we passed through a swinging door at the top, "I guess it worked out okay with your long-lost aunt?"

"Yeah, more or less."

"That was, what, two months ago?"

"And change."

"Wow." She nodded. "Time flies, huh?"

She asked what I'd been doing and I told her about Cuppa and Lennox as we walked the long, carpeted hallway. Finally she unlocked a wooden door near the end, holding it open for me.

"Beth said you wanted access to some records," she said as we sat on opposite sides of her desk. Behind her was a window, its blinds fully opened to let in as much sunlight as possible. The requisite diplomas were on the wall to her right.

"I do. My mother was a patient here before she died. Actually, I thought she was already dead, but turns out she wasn't."

"Well, some of the people here basically are." Petra clapped her hand to her mouth. "Oy. I'm sorry. I shouldn't have said that."

Still outspoken, I thought. "No problem."

"When was she here?" Petra asked, fingers tapping on the keyboard.

I gave her the year my mom died. "I'm not sure when she . . . checked in?"

"Last name?"

"Renfield."

She nodded, her fingers clicking quickly over the keys, then hovering lightly where they'd finished as she watched the flickering letters. "Yup. Georgia?"

There was a lump in my throat. They had it. "That's her," I said hoarsely.

"Some of her records are on the system. The rest are probably in the archives, handwritten. Barrow was just starting to file electronically then, so things in that time period are kind of a mishmash. Let's see what we've got . . ." She hit some more keys, glancing at me quickly. "You know, Beth down at reception is right, there really is procedure we're supposed to follow. Forms you need to file. I can tell you're anxious and I know you went to a lot of trouble to get here, so I'm going to tell you what I see, but I'll still need you to send in the paperwork and you won't be able to leave with anything—no notes, no photocopies, nothing— today. Is that cool?"

"That's great," I said. "Really. I appreciate anything you can tell me."

She shifted her eyes back to the screen. "Let's see . . ." She read for a minute or two, then looked up at me, her eyes wider. "She died here."

I nodded.

"You knew that?"

"It was in her obituary."

Petra nodded and resumed reading. "The cause of death is listed as . . ." She glanced at me and said softly, "Suicide. I'm sorry."

It shouldn't have been a surprise. I mean, she'd been at a mental institution. But it made me think of that girl, that awful day in New York, watching her fall. How must it have been for Nan? Awful to have her daughter run away, terrible that she wound up someplace like this. Unbearable to have her die like that. And then, suddenly, I realized Nan had come back here, remembered a few days with Agnes at our apartment and a woman, Mrs. Johnson, who sometimes stayed with me if Nan or Agnes had to go out. It was jumbled together, I was only six, but Nan had been tired when she came back. Didn't feel like playing Candyland or Chutes. Who would after burying their only daughter?

"How could that happen?" I asked. "Wouldn't she have been watched?"

"Yeah." Petra shrugged. "But we don't always see it coming and sometimes people are so determined . . ."

I nodded, thinking again of the girl in New York. "Does it say anything about her . . . problems? Why she was here?"

"Well . . ." Petra scanned the screen again. "She was at Barrow for about four years. Depression. Severe. But no details. That kind of stuff would be in the archives."

"Can we go there?"

She glanced at her watch, then nodded. "Okay. Just let me make a quick call."

I waited outside, hearing the soft mumble of her voice through the unlatched door. ". . . my final rounds? Owe you one." Then she was by my side. She gave my arm a little squeeze. "I really am sorry. I know how hard this kind of thing is."

I nodded, actually feeling comforted.

In the archives, cardboard boxes were stacked floor to ceiling on metal shelves. It took nearly half an hour of Petra's pawing through files to come up with my mother's.

"Whoa," she said, hefting a folder three inches thick from the box. She glanced at her watch again. "You came here by taxi, right?"

"Yeah."

"You have anyone picking you up?"

"No, I figured I'd just call for another taxi when I was done."

She nodded. "Well, I'm technically off now. My shift ended at five. We could sit here and sift through this or we could go through it at my place. My boyfriend, Wayne, is making dinner. If you don't mind his being there, it would be more comfortable and he's a great cook."

"Oh, no, I couldn't. Thanks, but . . ."

"You couldn't what? Come to my house? Have dinner?"

"Well, I don't want to put you out."

She shrugged. "How am I put out? If you don't come, I'm stuck in this basement well after I should be out of here." She stood, her knees cracking. "C'mon, let's go."

"I thought you said we couldn't take anything out of here, though."

"No," she said, grinning. "I said you couldn't."

Petra spent most of the ride talking about Wayne, her boyfriend. Also known as Wayne the Pain or Whiner Wayne.

"I mean, he has some wonderful qualities," Petra said, one hand twisting her dark hair while the other held the wheel. "That's why I was attracted to him in the first place. He's sweet and caring. The day after I went out with him for the first time, he hand-delivered a dozen roses to the hospital for me. Who does that?

"Of course," she continued, "he has lots of free time since he can't hold a job. It's always something—the hours, the environment, the boss—doesn't suit his 'artistic temperament.' He's moody too. I tried to avoid analyzing him when we first started dating, but I can't help it. I think he's manic-depressive. Maybe that's why I'm still with him. I keep thinking I can help, though I should know better . . ."

Her monologue was both entertaining and distracting, purposely so, I thought. I let her talk but found myself thinking of her black bag tossed in the backseat.

Finally we pulled into a dusty driveway beside a cute white clapboard house. A faded Toyota was already there.

"Home sweet home," Petra announced.

The porch sagged and the paint was rough, but Petra's house was completely charming. "What a great place. It's yours?"

"Nah, just renting. Not sure I'm ready to buy into Ridgevale just yet, but I do love the house."

Inside, it smelled wonderful—garlic and fresh herbs and onion. I hadn't eaten all day and, back at the hospital, would have thought it impossible, I was so keyed up, but I knew I'd be wolfing down whatever Wayne put in front of us. In fact, I hoped he was almost done.

"I brought a guest, Wayne," Petra called, hanging her keys on a Peg-Board beside the door.

A shaggy head poked around the corner.

"Hi." I waved. "I'm Cassie."

He wore a splattered apron and big smile as he came toward me. He was tall, lanky, very cute in a puppy-dog sort of way. I could see exactly what Petra meant about wanting to help him. His whole demeanor begged for a hug.

We shook hands and Petra gave him a peck on the cheek. "Smells great, babe," she said.

"It'll be done in about fifteen, twenty minutes."

Petra nodded. "Cassie and I are doing a little research. You mind if we get started, or do you need help?"

Wayne shook his head. "Nope, I've got it all under control."

He disappeared back into the kitchen and Petra dragged her bag into the living room, swinging it up onto a beat-up wooden chest in front of the sofa.

"We won't get through much," she said, pulling out the file, "but we can at least get our bearings before dinner."

I sat quietly, rethinking my desire to eat, anxiety churning in my stomach as Petra read. The living room was just big enough for a small slip-covered sofa, chair, and the coffee table chest. Everything was white or off-white: the walls, the furniture, the filmy curtains. Even the floors were a pale, weathered wood. It kind of surprised me. Being around institutional neutrals all day, I'd have thought Petra would opt for something more colorful. Or, given what I remembered from the plane, something a little more goth. This looked more country church than dank cathedral.

Through the archway, I saw Wayne adding a plate to the table before returning to the kitchen.

"Well . . . ," she said slowly. I sat forward, my hands gripping the cushion.

"Yeah? What do you see?"

She shook her head. "Not that much yet. She was admitted on recommendation from Bering General Psych Ward. Brought in by her mother."

"Nan," I whispered.

Petra nodded, still reading. "Right. Nanette Dinakis." She looked up. "Your grandmother."

"Yes."

She looked back at the file. "Looks like she was having episodes of depression that started about a month before." Petra paused, making eye contact again. "Right after the car accident that killed your father."

I nodded for her to continue.

"That's not unusual, you know. The admitting even noted it here. Losing a spouse, especially unexpectedly like that, is one of the toughest things a person can go through. The only thing worse is losing a child." Petra looked back at the pages. "Her depression must have been severe, though, for Bering General to have recommended her admittance to Barrow. The shortest stay for our patients is usually a month. They wouldn't have advised separating her from you, as young as you were and as much of a grounding influence as a child can be, unless they felt she was a danger to herself or maybe to you."

Wayne poked his head in then. "This is ready. You want me to hold off for a little?"

Petra looked at me and I said, "No, of course not. Let's go ahead and eat." I mustered a smile, adding, "It smells delicious."

I tried to relax as we sat at the table, a steaming plate of pasta in the middle. The dining room chandelier cast a warm glow throughout the room. Wayne and Petra exchanged stories about their day. He was sweet and I thought maybe Petra was a little hard on him, until he started talking about his last job. And the one before. I tried to join in the conversation, but I was eager to get back to the files. Petra must have sensed it, because as soon as we were finished, she stood.

"Fantastic meal, honey." She kissed the top of his head. "Let's clean up and then Cass and I need to get back to work."

"That's cool," he said, collecting plates while Petra brought the serving dish, and I, the glasses. "I think I'll go out to the porch, mess around with some tunes."

Once the dishes were loaded and table wiped down, Petra and I went back to our seats. Wayne had grabbed a guitar from the corner of the living room and through the doorway, I could hear his strumming, soft and pretty.

"He's not bad," I said quietly.

Petra nodded, her head still buried in the file. "No, he's not. I keep telling him that. He just needs to focus, start writing the songs down, putting words to them." She glanced up, smiling. "As you might have guessed, he doesn't take direction well."

She read for a while longer, then stretched, working her head side to side to loosen the muscles. "Okay," she said, resting her hands on her knees, within reach of the file on the coffee table. "It looks like your mom blamed herself for the accident. Survivor guilt. Again, not uncommon. Hers was more severe than most. Her doctor—a Mary Wells, who I met briefly when I first started at Barrow—also interviewed your grandmother Nan. Apparently she came to help out as soon as she heard about the accident. She stayed with you and your mom but could barely get your mom out of bed during the day. Then, at night, she'd find her walking the house, weeping, or watching over your bed. She got scared, unable to get Georgia—your mom—to talk to her at all. Nan says she just wasn't sure what was going through your mom's head, and when she took her into Bering General, they couldn't get much out of her either. Your mom was at Barrow for almost a month before she said anything during her sessions with Dr. Wells."

"Before she said anything? You mean she just sat there?"

Petra nodded. "Sure. That happens a lot. Patients are scared. It's very hard for some people to open up, especially if they've been through a trauma. Dr. Wells wasn't concerned. In fact, I can tell from her notes after she first met Georgia . . ." She paused. "Does it bother you if I call her that? It's how Dr. Wells referred to her."

I shook my head.

"Anyway, Dr. Wells expected it would take at least that long to get Georgia to talk."

"Okay, so then what? After a month, she started talking?"

Petra nodded. "I've only just read through their first session with any dialog. Dr. Wells had suspected depression, survivor guilt. That's obvious, given the situation, but this was the first time Georgia confirmed it."

"What did she say?"

Petra checked the handwritten pages again. "Very little. Dr. Wells asked Georgia if she was still sad. It's something she asked every time, sometimes getting a nod, others no response at all. This time Georgia nodded.

"'Can you tell me about it?' Dr. Wells asked.

"No response.

"'Do you miss Daniel?'

"Here, she nods again. Then she says, 'It's all my fault.'

"'What's your fault, Georgia?'

"'That he's gone.' She breaks down crying." Petra looked up. "That's it."

"That's it?"

"That was a real breakthrough, getting Georgia to confide at all. A chink in the armor."

I looked at Petra, then the file, only a fraction of the pages leafed through.

"This is going to take a while," Petra said, reading my thoughts.

"Your job requires a lot of patience," I told her.

"That it does."

"It's going to take you hours to read all of that." I felt guilty. I wanted to tell her she didn't have to. I mean, she'd be up until after midnight at the rate we were going, and I was sure she had to work the next day. But I was desperate to know what was in the file. "Can I help you sort through it?"

"No." She gestured to the pages. "Legally, I can't let you

without all the right forms. I's dotted, t's crossed and all that. But even if I wanted to bend the rules, I don't think it would help. Dr. Wells's notes are in a shorthand that wouldn't make sense to you."

She could read the disappointment on my face.

"Listen, Cass. I know you need to know what's in here. I don't mind reading it all, really I don't. I'm going to skim the session notes and see what I can find. Why don't you grab a book or even sit with Wayne for a while. I can fill you in as I go."

I should stay, I thought, still feeling guilty about letting Petra do all the work. But she was right, there was nothing I could do, and staring at her, waiting for each little tidbit, wouldn't help. "Maybe I'll sit outside for a bit. Get some air."

"Great idea."

I paused by the front door. "Thanks a million, Petra. I really owe you."

She smiled. "No sweat."

Wayne was leaning against the clapboard, barefoot, with his guitar across his lap.

"We could hear you inside," I told him when he finished playing. "Your songs are nice, very pretty."

"Thanks," he said. "I could hear you too."

I didn't say anything, embarrassed and a little annoyed.

"I didn't mean to," he said. "It's just real quiet out here."

I nodded. There was something so disarming about him. I could see why it was hard for Petra to make a break.

"Tough stuff about your mom," he added quietly.

"Yeah, well, I never really knew her. I'm just trying to figure out what happened."

"You're brave to do it," he said. "My old man walked out on us when I was five. My mom never told me why and I never asked. Don't think I'd want to hear it."

I shrugged. I wasn't sure I wanted to hear it either, but sometimes want and need are not congruent.

"I'm going to take a little walk while Petra's reading," I said. "Any recommendations about which way to go?"

He chuckled. "The roads around here are all pretty much the same. Cornfields, wheat fields, and more cornfields. Take your pick."

That sounded fine to me. I started walking.

Wayne was right, the road in both directions was long and straight, flanked by dry stalks of wheat. The sun was low in the sky and, in Ashville, would have been sinking below the hills already. Here it just hung perilously close to the flat horizon. It was warm, so I walked slowly. In no hurry.

It was awful to think about my mother, who I sometimes pictured as a younger Nan, sitting mutely, too sad to even talk about her sadness. She must have loved my father very much, I thought, unsure if having a wonderful thing while it lasted was any comfort.

I wished that I had been older and could have helped her somehow. Nan hadn't been able to, though. And, knowing Nan, she'd have tried her damnedest.

I wondered why she'd taken me back to Ashville rather than staying here. Or why Nan hadn't brought my mother to Ashville with us. Maybe Petra would find it in the files, the reason for putting half a country between mother and daughter. Then again, that might be one of those things I didn't want to know.

It was hard to imagine Nan out here. She liked being close to the beach, dipping her painted toes in the icy East Coast water, walking the boardwalks. Taking long drives, just to go. It would have been hard for her somewhere like this, with the view so unvaried. It had been perfect for me, a relief from almost the day I arrived, though I wasn't sure it was anymore. The luster had worn off with things fraying between Lucas and me, the fear of talking to another person with the mark, or running into that woman whose baby died.

I walked maybe a mile, until the sun was just above the wheat, spiny stalks teasing its bottom curve. Then I turned around and headed back, nervous but ready to hear what Petra had learned.

"I made good progress," she said, smiling and beckoning me to the couch when I got back. "The sessions were easy to read because a lot of it was repetitive. Georgia opened up very slowly. One step forward, two steps back. Then the same one step forward, you know?"

I nodded, plucking at my shirt, trying to cool down from my walk.

"I mean, there's still a lot here, but I'm through the first year at least. Georgia had survivor guilt all right, but it was unusual. Your mom felt responsible for the accident. Not just guilty that she survived, but she truly believed she could have prevented your father's death."

I felt a little shiver, the start of goose bumps on my still-sweaty skin. "How? I mean, was she the one driving? Did she distract him or something?"

"No, I don't think it was anything like that. There are no specifics in the notes about the accident itself. Dr. Wells didn't think

Georgia had full memory of it. Georgia actually believed she knew your father was going to die that day—had some kind of psychic pre-knowledge."

I felt very far away, as if I were looking at Petra through a long, long tunnel. "What do you mean 'psychic pre-knowledge'?" It took all I had to ask the question.

Petra didn't seem to notice. "I'm not sure. But that's not all that uncommon either, for survivors to think—looking back—that they had foreknowledge. They start to manufacture things that should have told them what was coming."

"Do you . . . Did Dr. Wells think that's what happened?"

"Well, that's the funny part," Petra said. "Georgia must have been very convincing. Dr. Wells was working on that theory, try-ing to make Georgia see that it wasn't her fault, that she couldn't have prevented the accident, but Georgia was adamant. She was completely certain that she knew, even swore that she tried to prevent it. She claimed she had warned your father ahead of time. I can see in Dr. Wells's notes that she did research on it, hadn't had that much direct exposure to this exact situation, but it seems that nearly every case she could find was distinctly different from your mother's."

"How so?" I was clinging to Petra's every word, hoping for something that might explain this all away and take me anywhere but where I felt sure we were heading.

"Her thinking that she had acted on her knowledge, for start-ers. Most of the time the guilt is for *not* acting. The other thing that was unusual is that your mother said there'd been others, other times she'd had this . . . knowledge. That's odd, Dr. Wells notes, the belief generally stemming from the traumatic incident

196 · JEN NADOL

and completely confined to it. In other words, survivors twist the facts immediately preceding the incident, but not other facts unrelated to it."

I was almost shaking now and Petra could see it: my hands clenched tightly together.

"Are you okay?" she asked, leaning forward. "Should I stop?"

"No, no. I want to hear it. Does Dr. Wells . . . does she say how my mother . . . what she saw or whatever that made her think she knew something?"

I held my breath, sure of the answer, waiting to hear it aloud.

"No." Petra shook her head. "Not in the ones I've read through so far."

Or any of the others, I guessed. It didn't matter; I knew. Far too well. "Is there anything else?"

"Yeah," Petra said. "She talked about you. . . . Are you sure you want to hear this?"

I nodded, afraid to speak.

"She was scared. Felt like she had to watch you constantly, but couldn't stand . . . well, it was hard for her to be there with you." Petra watched me as she spoke. "It happens a lot in cases like this too," she said. "After a trauma, people become convinced something bad is going to happen to other people they love. So much so, sometimes," she continued gently, "that they experience the heartbreak of it even before it happens."

"Is that why I was living with Nan?"

Petra nodded. "Georgia had a lot of guilt about that. She wanted so much to have you back, but every time she and Dr. Wells talked about the steps to get there, even to a halfway house, Georgia would withdraw more."

"Like she was afraid of it?"

"Right. Dr. Wells notes that it got to a point sometimes where she wasn't just afraid of how she'd protect you, but also of how to protect herself. She seemed preoccupied with death, always trying to prevent it, fearful of every action."

I nodded, thinking of how, over the last few months, I'd found myself wondering about every choice. How did it change my fate that, looking for my wallet in the morning, I was ten minutes later walking out my door than I would have been otherwise? Did I miss walking past a man, a dog, a bus that might change my life? Was that a good thing or not? If I wore pink socks instead of black, what would be the result? Would they attract the attention of the serial killer sitting next to me in the coffee shop? Were these things preordained or was I in control? You could drive yourself crazy with these questions. I guess my mother had.

Petra insisted I stay over. "You'll never get a cab out here at this hour," she said. I glanced at the clock, the hands hovering just past ten. "I'd drive you, but I've got a crazy day tomorrow."

I protested, but it was no use. She was right, I had no way home. Petra made me chamomile tea. "To help you sleep," she said. "Doctor's orders."

"You said you met Dr. Wells when you first started at Barrow," I said, the thought occurring to me as she was showing me to the guest room, also white on white. "Is she still there? Could we ask her about some of the details? Maybe she'd remember more—"

Petra cut me off with a shake of her head. "No. She died the year after I started. She was older, would have been in her late sixties when she treated your mother. The file seems pretty complete anyway," Petra added. "Dr. Wells had a reputation as a perfectionist. I'll keep looking. There are still another few years of sessions to read. Anything she learned from your mother is almost certainly in there. The rest, unfortunately, is not to be known."

The next morning Petra drove me to downtown Ridgevale. She knew of a bus service that ran to Bering twice a day.

"I'd have asked Wayne to take you," she'd said, "but honestly, I wouldn't trust his car to make it."

"Please, Petra, you've already been so great. I can't thank you enough. I owe you."

"Well, then repay me by keeping in touch. Maybe you haven't noticed, but there's a shortage of cool people out here," she said. "I try to make sure I know all of them."

"I definitely will."

"Good. Don't flake on me," she warned. "I have your number. I will track you down."

"No worries."

I slept a little on the bus ride, having gotten only broken sleep the night before, but my head kept spinning, trying to piece together the day of the accident. Had my mother been unable to convince my father about the mark? Lucas hadn't believed me, but we'd been dating less than a month. Was it possible that she hadn't told him? Or had she, the two of them rushing to the hospital, worried that it wasn't just a headache, but a stroke? An aneurysm? A tumor? I tried to imagine how I'd feel if the action I'd persuaded Lucas to take caused his death. The fated accident a slip in the bathroom rather than the skidding of brakes. Could that be what happened? Damned if you do, damned if you don't.

I'd never know the whole story, but I knew enough to believe that my mother, like me, could see the mark. And it had ruined everything.

"Where have you been? I've been worried about you. Tell me what happened—you saw another one, didn't you?"

Lucas showed up at Drea's apartment around four, frantic and petulant. I wasn't surprised to see him, though he'd never been up before. Drea wasn't due back until later, so I let him in reluctantly, wanting nothing more than to keep sipping tea and listening to Mozart, but I knew I had to deal with him eventually. I'd ignored all his messages and texts and thrown away the notes he'd taped to her door and slipped underneath it.

"I'm not doing it anymore, Lucas," I said, walking back to my mug by the sofa.

"What? You mean warning them? What happened? Another one who didn't believe you?" He folded his arms, preparing for another debate. "Well, don't forget about the one you saved."

"Yeah." I leaned forward to toss the paper at him, glad that I'd been too worn out to burn it or throw it away like I'd meant to. "I don't think I'll ever forget him."

Lucas scanned the paper, confused.

"That's him, Lucas. The guy in the picture. Eduard Sanchez."

I left the couch and walked to the window, staring outside at the slow-moving traffic while Lucas read.

"Cassandra . . ."

"I don't want to talk about it, Lucas. I'm done. I'm not meant to meddle. I know it doesn't make sense to you, but I feel it in my gut."

He said nothing.

I turned to face him, to make sure he understood me. This was it. No more discussions. No more arguments. This was a decision only I could make, and I felt sure I was making the right one.

"I can understand why you're upset," he said. "You should have called me."

I shrugged, turning back to the window. What I wanted was for Lucas to come to me, put his hands on my shoulders, tell me I was right, destiny was better left undisturbed.

Instead, he said, "I can see you need some time alone. I don't blame you. I think when you have more distance, time to sort through this, you might reconsider."

I didn't answer. There was nothing to say.

"I'll let myself out," he said softly.

chapter 26

I almost skipped class, but I felt I owed it to Professor McMillan to go. He'd been great, grading my exams and papers, though he wasn't required to for an audit student. He even wrote a nice note on my last one, saying what a pleasure it had been to have someone there purely for the joy of learning.

I was late, hoping it would prevent me from having to talk to Lucas. I felt his eyes on me the minute I walked into class, but I ignored him, sliding into the first empty seat and focusing on Professor McMillan, already lecturing. He was mid-sentence when Lucas's hand shot up.

"Yes, Lucas?" Professor McMillan turned to him, puzzled. I kept my eyes locked on my notebook.

"I was just thinking," Lucas said, "that it might be interesting to apply the readings on determinism and free will to the hypothetical Ms. Renfield brought up in one of our earlier classes." Lucas paused, adding pointedly. "Now that she's here."

He wouldn't dare.

"What hypothetical is that?" Professor McMillan asked.

"About the patient and the doctor. The patient thinks she's in good health, but the doctor finds something terminal." Lucas paused to look at me. He really was. He was putting my life up for debate. "Should the doctor tell? Does he have a responsibility to share what he knows?"

Professor McMillan thought for a minute, then nodded. "Very well. Why don't you lead the discussion?"

Lucas stood, a self-satisfied smile on his face. I closed my eyes, clenching my teeth as he repeated it: "What is the doctor's responsibility?"

Hands went up across the room.

"Determinists would say that the outcome is already decided," answered a blond girl, the one who'd called Lucas "choiceworthy." "Like, say it's heart disease. They'd say she was destined, from birth to have it. Maybe because the disease is in her genes or her mom brings her up on fatty foods or whatever. It's like it's fated— she never has a chance."

"Okay." Lucas frowned. "So, if it's all predetermined, fated, as you said, the doctor has no responsibility to try to help the patient?"

He wasn't looking at me, but he was talking to me. I was furious.

"No," the girl answered. "The doctor still has to tell."

"Why?" Lucas asked.

"Because he's *part* of the predetermined events. The patient's visit that day, the conversation they have, what they decide to do or not do—it's all part of the patient's destiny."

"Exactly." Lucas smiled approvingly. "So, even if he can't control the outcome, the doctor is still morally responsible for fulfilling his role and telling the patient, correct?"

She nodded, beaming.

"And what about the libertarians? How would they view this dilemma?"

"Well, they think *everything* is about choice, so the doctor definitely has to tell what he finds," a guy up front said. "If he didn't, he wouldn't be giving the patient a chance."

"Okay," Lucas said, "so again, the doctor has to tell."

I couldn't believe Lucas was doing this: twisting the lesson to suit his own agenda, making it seem like I had a moral duty to tell people about the mark. He was encouraging these flawed arguments and no one was calling him on it. Not even Professor McMillan.

"And finally," Lucas said smugly, "what would the compatibilists say?"

"Still the doctor's responsibility to tell," the same guy said. "I don't think there's any question about that in any of these arguments, the issue is really—"

Lucas cut him off, leaving me no doubt that this lesson was for no one but me.

I stood up. I was shaking, I was so angry. "First of all," I interrupted, several people nearby turning to stare, "determinists don't believe in moral responsibility and you know it, Lucas." More heads turned at my bluntness.

"Second, libertarians would say the doctor's only responsibility is to use his free will and choose the best solution—which might or might not be to tell—since *nothing* is predetermined."

I had everyone's attention now. "But it's a stupid question to start with. I mean, maybe I can buy the idea that a doctor, who *chose* his role and took a sworn oath to intervene, should tell someone that they're about to die. But of course we're not really talking about a doctor here."

I could sense my classmates looking at one another, confused. I never took my eyes off Lucas and he never took his off me. I tried to make my voice less strident, hoping one last time to get him to understand.

"I mean, we all know death is coming, right? We all have a chance to make the most of our time, to choose how we spend our days. There is a limit to them, it's not a secret. Why should anyone be responsible for giving you more than your share? Especially when there are no guarantees about what you'll do with them. Maybe it will be something good. Or," I said, thinking of Eduard Sanchez, "maybe it will be the opposite."

It was totally quiet in the room, every eye on me, notebooks and lesson abandoned. Professor McMillan had stood up, but he too waited, watching it play out.

"I'm not sure who I side with—determinists, compatibilists, whatever—but I believe Socrates was right that we are, each of us, responsible for our own happiness. You choose to smoke that cigarette, talk on that cell phone while driving, have that extra drink. You are responsible. In making those choices, you accept the outcome. Call it fate or personal accountability . . ." I shrugged. "It doesn't really matter."

I gave Lucas a minute to answer, but I could tell from the disappointment in his eyes that we were worlds apart. Always would be.

I collected my books and, the room still silent, walked out the door.

chapter 27

I went to the park. To the pond, my thinking place. I didn't really want to think, though. What I wanted was for all of this—the mark, my failed first love, Nan's lies about my mother—to go away. Be some kind of dream. Instead, it got worse.

I almost didn't answer my cell, sure it would be Lucas. It was Petra.

"You okay?" she asked almost immediately. "You sound bummed out."

"My boyfriend and I had a fight." In front of my philosophy class. About the meaning of my life.

"I'm sorry. I can call another time if you want . . ."

"No, no. What's up?"

"I finally finished reading the files. There was more in there. Some new stuff. You got a few minutes?"

"Sure." I lay back, feeling the tickle of grass against my neck, and closed my eyes. I didn't really want to hear anything else about my crazy mom and how she hadn't been able to handle the mark. If she couldn't, how could I? "Go ahead," I told Petra.

"Turns out there *was* more than just survivor guilt. About halfway through her second year, it started to come out. Dr. Wells believed it probably existed before the accident, in some form, but grew afterward."

"What grew?"

"Delusions." I could hear papers shuffling. "You ever hear of Lachesis?"

"Is that some kind of condition?"

Petra snorted. "Not even close. It's a person. *She's* a person, I should say."

The name, now that Petra identified it as one, was familiar, but just barely. I sat up, staring at the sparkly surface of the pond. "Who is she?"

"I looked it up to be sure," Petra said. "Lachesis," she read, "Disposer of Lots, one of the three Moirae. She measures the length of the thread of human life spun by Clotho."

"The three Moirae? What are Moirae?" But even as I asked it, I felt my stomach roll. I remembered where I had heard the name before. "Who is Clotho?"

"My questions exactly," Petra agreed. She continued reading. "The Fates, or Moirae, were Greek goddesses who controlled the destiny of everyone from the time they were born to the time they died. They were: Clotho, who spun the thread of a person's life; Lachesis, the apportioner, who decided how much time each person was allowed; and Atropos, the inevitable, who cut the thread when you were supposed to die."

Petra kept reading. "The Fates were often depicted as cold and unmerciful, but weren't always deaf to the pleading of others.

When Atropos cut the thread of King Admetus, Apollo begged the Fates to undo their work. They promised that if someone took Admetus's place in the gloomy world of Hades' domain, he would live."

I remembered Nan sitting with me, both of us leaning against my headboard, I in my pajamas, she with a well-worn book open before us. Sometimes she didn't even need the book.

"Cassie? Hello? You still there?"

"I'm still here," I croaked.

"So you're probably wondering what this has to do with your mother."

"Right." My head was spinning. I tried to focus on the pond, the trees, anything real and concrete to anchor the things swirling in my brain. The memories, the stories, the facts that were adding up way too fast.

"Your mother believed she was a direct descendant of Lachesis, one of the Fates. The one who determines the length of a human life. She had constructed a whole world of facts to fit her beliefs. Dr. Wells only uncovered parts of it, even in their years of therapy. She was certain Georgia's delusions ran deep. Some of the things she spoke about went way back."

"Like what?"

Petra paused and I could hear more pages shuffling. "Remember how she said she'd known before when someone was going to die? There was a friend of hers in high school . . ." I heard Petra flipping pages again, but saved her the time, my whole body numb.

"Roberta." The reason she'd run away. The bee sting. I could hardly think, unable to believe it hadn't occurred to me before and unwilling to imagine it was true.

"Right! Roberta Bikakis. How did you know?"

"Just heard her name before, I guess."

"Yeah. Anyway, she was a friend of your mother's who died when she was sixteen. Your mother claimed she knew before it happened." Petra paused. "Your family's Greek, right?"

"Right."

"People don't usually pick these things out of thin air," Petra said. "There's always a source of the delusions. Your mom probably drew on the things she heard, or was taught at church." I could picture Petra shaking her head in a sorry admiration. "Dr. Wells had to research the mythology to understand what Georgia was talking about. Your mother certainly knew her stuff. She constructed a very solid fantasy world."

If only that were it, I thought. "What else did she . . . do the notes say about it?"

"Not much," Petra answered. "Georgia was pretty tight-lipped, only dropping bits and pieces. In one session, Dr. Wells was questioning her about why she felt responsible for your father's accident and she answered, 'I am fate.' That was it. Then it's another two months before Georgia let the name Lachesis slip. The thing that struck Dr. Wells was how firmly Georgia held to her beliefs. Her facts never changed, never conflicted. Though Dr. Wells never got the full story, she was sure there was a whole construct beneath the surface that Georgia held tight to."

"Uh-huh." It came out like a punch in the gut, which was pretty much how I felt.

"The other thing," Petra continued, "and this is what made me think she got the ideas from something she was taught, was that Georgia mentioned a book."

There were goose bumps on my arms. "What book?"

"Hold on. I've got it in the notes somewhere." More pages

shuffling. "Here it is," Petra said. "It was late in their sessions, only a month or two before your mom died. Dr. Wells was trying to get her to share more of her beliefs about her ability to predict death." Petra paused, reading. ". . . and also about her being a descendant of this Lachesis.

"'How can you be sure of this?' Dr. Wells says.

"'It's in the book,' Georgia answered.

"'What book?'

"Georgia only shook her head. .

"'What book, Georgia?'

"'I can't tell.'

"'Why not?'

"'My mother told me not to.'

"'Was it one of her books?'

"'It's ours. Meant for us alone, until she's sixteen.'

"'Until who's sixteen, Georgia?'

"'I'm not sure I'll give it to her. I'm supposed to, but I don't think I will. I wish it hadn't been given to me.'

"And that's it," Petra said.

"That's it?"

"Yeah. Dr. Wells notes that Georgia was unresponsive to further questions. At first I thought the book might be one of your father's. He was a history professor, right?"

"Ancient history." He'd have known the myths, the stories of the gods and godesses. Could have helped a scared sixteen-year-old sort things out, maybe better than her own mother.

"When I reread the notes, though, it seemed pretty clear the book belonged to your grandmother Nan. And Georgia was probably talking about you, right? With the whole 'until she's sixteen'?"

"I guess."

"That's what Dr. Wells assumed. She tried to bring it up with Georgia at their next session and after that too, but she never got any further. And then . . . it ended."

It ended. My mother checked out. Decided it was all too much.

"Was there anything more?" I asked Petra. "Anything about her . . . ability? Specifics, like what she thought she could do or see?"

"No. You know, Cassandra, your mother was pretty heavily medicated throughout. Dr. Wells tried getting her to talk about the delusions so they could work through them, she tried focusing on the positives—on you—to encourage Georgia to work toward reality, but truthfully there wasn't a lot of progress in the three or four years she was at Barrow."

Petra was silent, thoughtful for a minute, then added, "I'm sorry, Cassie. I know this must be hard to hear, even if you never really knew her."

So much harder than Petra could ever know. "Thanks. For everything, Petra."

"No problem. Keep your promise, Cass. Stay in touch."

chapter 28

I hung around Bering for a day or two after that, but I had no job, no school, didn't dare go out for fear of seeing the woman with the baby or Lucas or anyone from class.

I desperately wished I could rewind back to the day I decided to visit my parents' grave and stay safely tucked in the apartment instead. To make things right, though, I'd need to rewind further, back to when I saw the mark on Lucas. Or maybe to the rainy day I followed Mr. McKenzie. But there's never a way to go back, so I did the only thing I could. Go forward.

Drea and I had talked when she got home from her business trip. Yeah, she'd known my mother survived the accident, assumed I'd known too. She'd visited her once at Barrow.

"I didn't live here, but I was back for my mom's funeral," she said. "I knew Mom would have wanted me to check in on Georgia. She always liked your mother, the daughter I should have been maybe." Drea looked away. "I don't even know if she recognized me, Cassie. She didn't say a word the whole time, and she looked . . ." She caught herself, remembering that this was my mother; what she said would be some of the only real memories I'd have of her. "Well, not herself. I never went back. Ashamed to say I didn't even come for her funeral." Drea shook her head and, for once, seemed truly remorseful. "I guess I'm just not that great at keeping in touch. Maybe just not that great . . . with people, in general. I know I've been kind of a lousy guardian."

"It's okay, Drea," I told her. "You were just what I needed." It was more or less the truth.

We parted amicably. I had a few days left with her, but I was ready to go and she said she wouldn't stand in my way. We left with hollow promises to keep in touch, but who knew? Maybe we would. She was family, after all.

Agnes's nephew John met me at the Ashville airport.

"You look tired, Cassie," he said.

I nodded. "I am."

The apartment was exactly as I remembered: throw blanket on the sofa, boxes in the hallway, mail tossed haphazardly on the foyer table, Nan's door firmly closed. Everything just as I'd left it three months before.

My overnight bag slid from my shoulder and, out of habit, I tossed it toward my room. It landed with a thud in the uneven nook by my door, where I'd always kept my backpack. The sight and feel of so much familiar still hurt. Slowly I walked into the living room and to the window, looking out at Miller's Pond, as rippled and shimmery as the one in Bering had been.

I stood there for a while, staring, thinking of nothing and

everything. Then I went to my room and slept for the next nineteen hours.

After I'd rested, I searched the bookshelves. The book Nan had given me eight months before, on my sixteenth birthday, was there, waiting, just as I'd remembered. It was smaller than today's paperbacks, yellowed and handwritten in Greek letters, like the ones on the fraternity houses at Lennox. It had to be the one my mother had mentioned. Too coincidental that Nan had given it to me, a book I couldn't read, with no explanation, on my sixteenth birthday. I thought about throwing it away, maybe lighting it on fire and tossing it in the tub or sink to burn. But I'd come too far, knew too much already not to put the final pieces together.

I called around a couple places. Finding a Greek scholar in Ashville, Pennsylvania, isn't the easiest thing, but I finally came up with a professor at the local college who was willing to take a look at it.

I met him at his office an hour later.

"It's old," Professor Laukaitis told me. "And not well preserved. I'll do my best, but it'll take at least a few days. Maybe a week."

"Fine." I gave him my number and went back to the apartment to wait.

On my third day home, I went into Nan's room. I could still catch the faintest hint of her smell—fresh grass and lilies—and imagine her sitting cross-legged on the bed, hunched over a book or crossword.

I was angry at her. Almost numb with fury. I'd been disappointed hearing things from Drea that Nan had never shared, but I understood. I could even forgive her, I thought, for lying about my mother's death and the mental hospital. But this I couldn't get past—that she had known about the mark, what it meant and why I saw it, and never told, never tried to help.

I went through her boxes, thinking I might find something to explain it. There were pictures of me as a little girl: in a sandbox, at Christmas, holding tightly to Nan's hand. There were letters she'd saved, cards I'd given her through the years. There was little about my mother and father, nothing I hadn't already discovered. The boxes were mostly our memories, hers and mine. Nothing useful.

I spent the rest of the day packing, filling box after box that I'd picked up on my way home from Professor Laukaitis's office. I started in the kitchen, feverishly piling pots, pans, dishes, towels, working as hard as I could to keep my mind blank and make my body tired enough for sleep.

Sorting the things of our life into bags for Goodwill and boxes to keep took the better part of two days. I was almost done when Professor Laukaitis called.

Two hours later I was back in the apartment, an envelope of neatly typed pages held tightly in my hand. He'd wanted me to stay, read them there so we could talk. I escaped with a promise to call another day. A promise I knew I would break.

I'd been desperate to look at the translation on the bus ride home, but too fearful of what it would say to risk doing so in such a public place. Now, in the quiet of the apartment, I sat on the chair in our half-packed living room and closed my eyes. I took a deep breath and held it, clearing my mind, knowing that the next minutes would change my life forever. Then I exhaled and began to read.

Daughter,

On the eve of my sixteenth year my own dear mother shared the history of our family with me. It is this that I wish to share in kind with you, as my mother instructed.

In ancient times our people believed that the course of a man's life was decided by rule of the Moirae—Clotho, Lachesis, and Atropos. These sisters—the three Fates— wed and had children who carried with them the gifts of their lineage.

We are of that lineage, descended from the Fate Lachesis, responsible for deciding the length of the thread of life.

I cannot say how our gift will manifest itself in you or whether it will at all. It is likely you will know yourself, have been aware of it long before you read these words or hear them from my own lips. All I can tell you is that, if you are given the power, you will know the day of a man's death and may choose to share that knowledge, changing the course of what might be.

As in ancient times, the balance of man and days must be maintained. For every life granted, another is denied. For every soul extended days, another is cut short. We must decide when to shift the course of events, but with the utmost care and deliberation and full acceptance of responsibility and limitation.

There are others, those with the blood of Clotho, Atropos, their brother Thanatos, and perhaps more of the ancient ones, so said my mother. I have yet to encounter one, though I have watched, waited, even searched as much as my limited circumstances could allow. Still, I believe they must exist. I long to find one with which to share this burden, not just in words, but in action. Separated, our abilities to choose wisely are, by nature, limited, as each ancient Fate relied upon another to augment and inform her work.

You, my beloved daughter, hold in the palm of your hand the gift and curse of granting another day, another year, another lifetime. This responsibility troubles my mind ceaselessly. I continue to try to fulfill our duties, though I worry it will be the very death of me.

Though you are but ten, I commit these words, our story, to these pages so that should I not be here to hold your hand and look into your dark eyes on your sixteenth birthday as my mother did, you will still know what you have inherited, gift and responsibility.

Your loving mother,
Helene Diodinis

I let the pages—not a book at all, but a letter written in a journal, century-old advice that could have been from my own doomed mother to me—lay in my lap. I stared across the room at the spot where Nan used to sit, where I had told her about the mark and she'd let me believe I was the only one with this awful ability.

Later, I'm not sure how long after, I walked to the foyer, skirting the stacks of boxes, to reach the door. There was one more visit to pay.

chapter 29

My cab turned into the long drive of the cemetery past the church where Nan's funeral had been held.

"Which way?" the driver asked.

"Up the hill."

It was raining. Not an ugly, pelting downpour, but a light summer shower. Tears of the gods, Nan's mother had called it. I remember her telling me that as we sheltered under an old oak in the preserve, caught by surprise during a walk. It must have been three or four years ago. Had she been sharing a memory or trying to say something more?

"Stop here." I recognized the gentle slope of the hill and the dark obelisk that stood just behind Nan's grave. The driver had agreed to wait despite the ready fares the weather would bring. I got out, rain sprinkling my face, and trudged up the incline to the hard block of stone bearing her name, NANETTE DINAKIS, and the dates of her life in the unremarkable font of a newspaper or novel.

There were fresh flowers by some of the graves, but Nan's was bare. Just me and her. I didn't want to sit. Not because the ground was wet or I knew I'd get dirty, but because I didn't want to be close to her. She hadn't trusted me. She'd told me she did, but her actions said otherwise.

"I'm here, Nan," I said, my voice loud and angry in the quiet of the graveyard. "I've been gone for a while. Three months. I moved to Kansas. Bering, of all places." I looked around the deserted cemetery, trying to rein in the emotions that felt ready to boil over. "Of course, you know that already. You sent me there."

I took a deep breath and ran a hand across my face, wiping away the rain. "I went to their graves. That's what you wanted me to do, right? Find out the things you were too chicken to tell me yourself?"

It was the only explanation for her sending me to live with Drea. I shook my head, feeling my fingernails digging angrily into clenched hands.

"I can't believe you never told me, Nan. About what really happened to my mother. But mostly about the mark. How could you listen to me after I watched Mr. McKenzie die and pretend you knew nothing about it?" My bangs were clinging to my forehead, dripping rain into my eyes just as they had that day. She'd given me a warm towel. So much easier than the truth.

"And those West Lakes kids . . ." All these years later, I could still remember them so clearly, kids playing ball, laughing, running. By nighttime, they were dead. "I was only four, Nan. I didn't know what I was seeing, but you did." I shook my head again. "That's not who I thought you were.

"Of course, I knew that girl in New York was going to die." I admitted softly, "And I let her. So maybe I'm no better."

I sat finally, tired of standing, my anger seeping out, like the rain running silky trails down my neck. I didn't even bother spreading my jacket on the wet ground.

"Was it Roberta Bikakis that changed you? Was it your idea to keep her in the apartment that day? My mother's? Or did you decide together like you and I used to? Of course, our decisions were about trivial things like what color to paint the living room. Hardly life and death. You couldn't trust me with that."

I remembered thinking, fleetingly, after I'd saved Lucas how devastated I'd have been if I'd convinced him to stay where the greatest harm waited. Exactly what had happened with Roberta. No wonder my mom ran away.

"I can imagine why you didn't want to use the mark after that," I said. "But maybe there's a reason it happened that way. Or maybe you just messed up, but could have saved others if you hadn't quit, ones who should have been saved.

"If you'd told me, we could have figured it out together. Am I fate? Were you? Or was the woman who wrote that letter just crazy? My mom too. And what am I supposed to do with this . . . this gift?" The word felt sour on my lips. It's what Lucas had called it. I thought the woman who wrote the letter had said it better with *curse*. What must it have been like for her, worried that she wouldn't live to share her secrets with her daughter? The mark too much of a burden, overtaking her life, just as it had my mother's.

"Maybe," I said softly, trying out an idea that hit me as I spoke to Nan's silent headstone just like I'd spoken to my mother's twelve hundred miles away, "maybe you were just too afraid. Worried that you'd lose me like you'd lost your daughter."

As soon as I said it, of course, I knew it was true. I remembered the boxes in her room where I'd looked for clues—letters or a journal—anything that would explain her mind, why she'd with-held the truth. I'd been looking right at it, I realized, holding the pictures and mementos of our life. It wasn't that Nan had thought the mark shouldn't be used or that she hadn't trusted me—she hadn't trusted herself, having already failed once.

"I would never have left you," I told her, staring at my hands clenched in my lap. "Nothing you told me could have made me go. I've missed you every day since you've been gone. Even today." I saw a tear drop onto my thumb, disappearing immediately on the slick of my rain-drenched skin.

Sitting by Nan's grave, I could remember a hundred things about her. The way her brow knit while she helped me with home-work, how she taught me to make tea, working in the kitchen so fluidly without a motion wasted, the pride on her face at my grade school graduation. I knew what Nan had done, the things she'd withheld, was because she had loved me.

I stood, brushing wetness from the folds of my clothes where it had collected. "I'm going to go now, Nan. I'm not sure where, but it may be a while before I'm back. A long while." I took a step closer to the headstone, running my hand over the arched top, hop-ing to feel something of Nan. But of course, it was just cold, hard marble. Nothing like the woman I'd known.

"I love you, Nan," I told her, closing my eyes and turning my face to the sky, letting the rain beat down as I listened one last time for anything, any part of Nan.

It was probably just the wind and rain hitting the stones around me, but walking down the hill to my waiting cab, I thought I finally heard her. Or maybe it was just my own inner voice, the one that was my guide all along, repeating her trademark phrase: *What now?*

I climbed into the back of the taxi, wishing I knew.

chapter 30

The first day of school. The first day of the rest of my life. It was surreal, walking through the doors of Ashville High again. I hadn't been gone that long, but felt like I'd gone really, really far. I'd forced myself to come back here, hoping it might make me feel normal again. I really needed that.

"Cassie!" Tasha ran down the hall grinning, her hair cut short in a sleek bob. She looked older, but in a good way. Not the way I felt. She grabbed me in a tight bear hug. "I've been trying to get you. You've been back for days. Why didn't you call?"

"Sorry, Tash. I've been swamped."

"What've you been doing?"

"Oh, you know . . ." Yelling at my dead grandmother, packing up the apartment like I have someplace to go, trying to decide if I'm fate or just fated for the asylum. "Sorting through stuff. Getting my bearings."

"Yeah, it must be weird to be back."

"Understatement of the year." The idea of sitting through

classes, trying to pretend any of this mattered . . . I kept trying to convince myself I could make it work, but I felt totally off, like the latch on my old locker, bent in a way so it never quite snapped into place. There were a few things I'd honestly been looking forward to, though. Seeing Tasha was one of them.

"Well, I'm glad you're back," Tasha said, tucking a sweep of hair behind her ear. "I have soooo much to tell you, but first I want to hear about Kansas and your aunt. And your boyfriend! Oh my God, Cassie, what a crazy summer you had!"

"Yeah, it was." Literally.

Tasha nudged my arm. "C'mon, let's find our lockers. You can tell me about it on the way. Where's yours?"

I looked at the slip of paper telling me what to do, a relief to have this small part of my life mapped out so clearly. "Just down the hall. Three fifty-one."

Tasha frowned. "I'm downstairs. One twenty-two. Who do you have for homeroom?"

"Milchuck."

"We're not together," she said. "I've got Mrs. Allen."

"Yeah, I saw you weren't on my list." I'd also seen who *was*, my breath catching when I thought of seeing him again.

Ashville High looked the same as when I'd left in May, the gray linoleum floors shiny but still not quite clean, tiled walls, kids lingering by their lockers smiling, whispering, picking up right where they'd left off.

"So? Tell me about Lucas," Tasha urged. "I got all your e-mails. I'm sorry we didn't get to talk more . . ."

"That's okay."

"It sounded so intense! Was it hard to leave? Are you going to see him again?"

I shook my head. "We broke up."

"What?! Oh my God, Cassie." She stopped, grabbed my arm. "What happened?"

If I'd been thinking straight these past few days, I'd have come up with something to tell her. It was obvious we'd come to this. I could say it was an argument, but Tasha would never leave it at that. She'd think I was nuts if I told her it was about a philosophy lesson and probably even more nuts if I explained why that lesson mattered.

"Hello? Cass?"

"I'm sorry, Tasha." I smiled weakly. "I'm a little out of it."

"No shit." She crossed her arms, waiting. "So? What happened?"

"Oh." I sighed. "Long story." Tasha frowned. This was the kind of thing best friends shared, but there's no way I could tell her. Not all of it. "It's way too much to get into here. We'll talk later."

"Well, are you okay?" We started walking again. Tasha was still frowning, but seemed more worried than annoyed.

"Sure," I said. "It wasn't meant to be. I'm over it."

Tasha stopped again and looked at me hard. "No you're not."

"No," I said, actually smiling. This is what I loved about Tasha. "I'm not. But I will be."

We'd reached my locker and Tasha leaned against the wall while I twirled the knob, setting the combination. The door clicked open smoothly.

"Works," I said, shutting it. I had nothing to put in there, but they made us check them anyway. "Should we do yours?"

"Yeah." We walked down the stairs and toward her locker, Tasha telling me about the summer in Ashville, the boy she'd worked with, weekend trips to the beach, concerts. It sounded so nice. Ordinary.

Classmates passed us, waving and nodding. I smiled back, trying to be happy about being back here, among friends. Trying to
look as sane as Tasha or as any of them. Trying not to notice the
way they looked when they walked through the shaft of sunlight
streaming in the window—as if they were marked. They weren't.
Not today.

The bell rang just as we got to Tasha's locker.

"Ugh! I can't believe school's starting again already," she said.
"You'd better get upstairs. Want to come over later today? You
can stay for dinner, my mom's making tacos."

My fave. "Sure."

"I'm glad you're back, Cass," Tasha said, punching my arm
lightly. "I missed you."

"Yeah, me too." I *had* missed Tasha and our lazy afternoons at
her house, runs for coffee at Jake's. I didn't know if we could ever
go back there, though. I was a different person now. Of course, so
was she. That's part of what William James was saying with the
whole Divinity Street thing Lucas and I had talked about in his
apartment: none of us are ever who we were yesterday.

I jogged the rest of the way down the hall and up the stairs to
Mr. Milchuck's room, passing lockers and a string of posters that
seemed to shout at me, squeezing through the door of my new
homeroom just before final bell.

The only seat was in the front row. I grabbed it, wishing I
could turn around, but too nervous to look for the only person I
really wanted to see. Afraid that maybe I'd read him wrong or
that he'd gotten back with Val while I'd been gone.

Instead, I kept my eyes locked on the blackboard, MR. MIL-
CHUCK written across it in large block letters, just like the
first day of philosophy. I felt further than ever from answering

Professor McMillan's question. And I wasn't even looking for the metaphysical, but something much more straightforward. Am I Cassie Renfield, descendant of the gods, or just a girl at the end of a long line of crazy people?

Announcements started. Hamburgers for lunch, cheerleading tryouts next week, tees and sweats for sale after school. I stood with the rest of the class to recite the Pledge, words tumbling effortlessly from my lips. Liberty. Justice. The posters I'd passed on the stairs—Responsibility, Honesty, Choices. I don't know why they even put that stuff up. No one pays attention. I never had before.

Socrates said the unexamined life is not worth living. Maybe. But it's probably a lot more fun.

The bell rang again. Time for class. I stood, slinging my backpack over my shoulder, waiting for the kids ahead of me to file through the door and trying my darnedest to be what I hoped I looked like—a girl, sixteen going on seventeen, with worries no deeper than guys and good grades.

I was so tired of thinking about the mark, what was right, was wrong. My duty, if I had one. I was afraid. Not just of seeing it and having to decide what to do. Or of the awful confrontation. That all sucked, but mostly I was afraid that I would never fit in somewhere like this again. I feared the same thing as Nan. Being alone. Could I ever find someone to tell my secret to who would still treat me like me?

"Cassie?"

He was right behind me, so close that when I turned, my shoulder brushed his arm, my heart tightening.

"Hi."

Jack smiled gently. "Hi," he said. We stared at each other for a minute, our classmates and friends plodding past. He was wearing that same sweatshirt, the one he'd worn the day he walked me home from school after Nan died. I remembered how he'd been then—solid, reassuring. And the way he'd looked at me when we met in Wichita, the way he was looking at me now.

Maybe, I thought. Just maybe.

"You have a good summer in Kansas?" Jack asked.

"It was . . . interesting." I smiled so he wouldn't take it as seriously as it sounded.

"We should get to class, but I'd like to catch up," he said, direct as always. "We never really got a chance to talk this summer. I don't know if you're free . . . or want to . . . but maybe we could meet up after school?"

"I'm going to Tasha's today," I said. "Can we do it tomorrow?"

"Definitely." We smiled at each other, neither of us sure what to do next. Maybe in no hurry to find out. Things with Lucas had been intense. I wasn't ready to jump back into that. Jack glanced at his watch. "We should go." At the door, he paused. "I'm glad you're back, Cassie."

"Me too." In that moment, I was.

Jack ran up the stairs to his class, but I walked to mine, slower than I should have. The halls were empty and I'd be late, but I didn't care. I wanted these minutes alone, passing the classrooms where I'd sat when I didn't even know what the mark meant. Before Mr. McKenzie. While Nan was still alive and I'd been so sure of who she was, of who I was.

I didn't know if being back here would make it harder or easier to figure it all out. The questions had only gotten tougher, more complicated. Maybe that's the way life always is.

I've learned, though. I know what the mark means now and I know I have the power to use it. Beyond that, like Socrates, the only thing I really know is that I know nothing.

But I'm going to find out.

many thanks to . . .

• my dedicated and diligent agent, Jenoyne Adams, for your enthusiasm and tireless efforts

• my editor, Caroline Abbey, for your thoughtful guidance and terrific eye, making this story far stronger than it was

• my husband, Joe, for your support, encouragement, and the key suggestion

• my parents and sisters—Ann, Anthony, Caitlin, and Noreen Rearden—who read, encouraged, and always believed

• everyone at Bloomsbury Children's Books whose hard work transformed *The Mark* from a file on my computer to a real, live book (holy cow!)

• all the others who read some or all of this manuscript— especially Elisabeth West, who is both a great friend and a great sounding board—for your help along the way

• and finally, my sons—Joey, Sam, and Jacob—who taught me the value and brevity of time and inspired me to do more